By **Flinty Maguire**

Trouble at the Crab Shack Café
Ellie Booton's Journal, No. 1

The Lighthouse Code
Ellie Booton's Journal, No. 2

The Abandoned Rule Book
Ellie Booton's Journal, No. 3

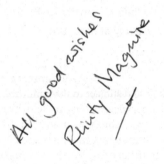

In this book you'll see an occasional asterisk *
This means there's an extra jot at the back.

For more information about Flinty Maguire

www.flintymaguire.com

First published in Great Britain by Burdock House, 2019

British Library Cataloguing in Publication Data
A CIP catalogue record for this book is available from
the British Library.

ISBN: 978-0-9930984-5-1

Thank you...

Patrick, who grew into my best friend, ever, and who gifts me ideas all the time.

Brontë, our Labrador, who is in my mind when I write about Herman; and Pippy, our rescue. They show me how imperfectly sound they are every day.

Jack and Fin, the non-fictitious boys in my life who are entirely unique and wonderful. Thank you for letting me borrow your names, and love to your fab parents who planted you on this earth.

Eden, my talented young friend. Thanks for inspiring me with your name. If only your politeness had transferred to the Eden in this book!

Thank you, Ian Harvey, staff and supporters of Congo Children Trust, for your dedication to the children of Kimbilio. Love to all the Kimbilio* children.

Thank you, Father Jonathan and folks of St. Margaret's Church, and the staff and children of St. Peter's Primary School, and Badger Hill, in the village of Brotton, North Yorkshire, for your support for Kimbilio.

Here's the good news - swiftly followed by childish, obnoxious behaviour

It's sunny. School is OUT.

I'm FREE!

Confused by this euphoria? Let me tell you something: sunshine in England is never taken for granted, especially if you live at the coast. Ever heard of south westerlies or sea frets? Well, neither had I until I came to live here. So, when the sun's out, we get excited – and when you've got a clear run at the summer holidays with no problems in sight, life seems just about perfect.

Let's see. General plans? There are NO pesky school projects to worry about – BRILLIANT! Jack's coming to stay with his laugh-a-lot Auntie Maggie. We'll have barbeques. We'll go sailing in Eddie's new boat. It's going to be endless hours of fun and relaxation. I'm seriously chilled.

Hang on. Mum's calling. Back in a mo...

And now for the bad news. That didn't take long.

Am in SHOCK. Life STINKS.

Old news: Dad's latest book – actually selling and making money.

VERY recent news: He's going to America to promote it. It's a wonderful, totally unexpected, out of the blue invitation – *apparently*. First thoughts on hearing this? *OK, off you pop. Send me a postcard.*

I was flippant. I noticed Dad looking a bit shifty. Then I looked at Mum and she looked away.

I think I said, 'What's wrong, Mum? This is great news, right?'

Great news for some... Dad's not flying solo. Mum and my sticky little brother are going to America too. I am not. In that split second, I became the kid who is left home all alone.

After a choking episode, I gasped, *'What?'*

'The timing's unfortunate, Ellie,' gulped Mum, avoiding eye contact. 'We'll be gone for six weeks. We can't take you because you'd miss the start of autumn term.'

'You're *ABANDONING* me?'

'Of course not. You won't be alone. You'll have Grandma and Eddie.'

'Eddie?' I spluttered. You'll know that Eddie is my big-ape brother. 'Is this some sort of *sadistic* joke?'

I felt awful saying that. I am the apple of Grandma's eye and she's always good company. Eddie, on the other hand, stinks.

Mum asked me if I was OK. She tried to hug me. I twisted away and snapped, 'Do I *look* OK?'

Dad was less sympathetic. He asked me when I had become such an obnoxious kid.

I replied with something obnoxious. Then I made my exit by slamming the kitchen door. Hard.

A storm cloud in the shape of voluminous baggy pants has appeared on the horizon; pants that have been hung out to dry, to block the sun and to shame me.

By 'PARENTAL ORDER'

Quelle surprise! Another GIGANTIC shock. My parents have been plotting against me. They've written a 'rule book' to keep me 'sound' while they're away.

'A bit of light reading,' says Dad, thwacking it down on the kitchen table. He grins and flashes a pile of paper stuffed into a tatty envelope labelled:

F.A.O. Ellie Booton

This is your "All Alone and Abandoned" Rule Book.

How very, very patronising. I hate the quotation marks. I never said I was going to be 'all alone and abandoned.' A kid would say that. I didn't. I'm sure I didn't.

Yes, we are leaving you but, no, we're not abandoning you, and you won't be all alone. The title is ironic. However, these rules MUST BE FOLLOWED and STRICTLY ADHERED TO, BY PARENTAL ORDER.

Compiled by Walter Booton, devoted dad to three offspring, otherwise known as the Three Bootoneers

And in Mum's writing:

- and Flora Booton, mother of darling aforesaid children.

Also known as Mum xoxox

What a con. If I were so *darling*, they'd take me with them.

The kitchen is in chaos. They must have been secretly packing for months – there are suitcases and bags everywhere. I'd throw myself on the floor and beat it with my fists, but there's no room.

'Get a move-on, Walter. We don't want to miss the flight,' says Mum.

Dad fastens his crime-against-fashion sandals and I wonder if America is ready for him.

'Exactly how many rules are there?' I ask, coldly.

'Forty-nine,' quips Mum, fixing her lipstick. She's wearing Bermuda shorts and an orange T-shirt that says, HAPPY TRAVELLER with a winking emoji. If she's sad about leaving me, she's disguising it well. Orange is her happy colour.

'Fifty, actually,' chirps Dad. 'We rounded it up.' He flashes me a big, cheesy grin.

I swallow, nervously. 'Like a rule a day?'

'Ha!' Dad eyeballs me over his glasses. 'A rule a day would mean we'd be away for seven weeks and one day. Which is...'

'*Incorrect,*' I snap, 'because you'll *only* be gone for six.' I pause for dramatic effect, then add, '*Unfortunately.*'

'I'm sorry, Ellie,' says Mum. 'We want to take you but it's just not possible.'

'Oh sure,' I say. 'Missing a few days of school would ruin my *entire* life... Couldn't we pretend I was sick?' I plead.

'It's against the law,' says Mum.

'And child cruelty isn't? You're leaving me with *Eddie!'*

Eddie looks a bit hurt.

'It will be good for you to rely on one another a bit more,' says Dad.

'O-M-G,' I say, slowly and deliberately. I know Mum hates me saying that. I throw her a raggy look and her lip begins to quiver. Mum's depression has lifted, but her mood can still see-saw, and for a long time she wore grey.

'I won't go. I don't know *what* I was thinking,' she says, slumping in a chair.

Herman, our Labrador, is a body language expert. He pins back his ears and looks anxiously at Mum. Then he looks at me. Everyone is still.

I speed-think things through. I don't want Mum to go back to sitting at the kitchen table staring at her hands.

I surprise myself by muttering, 'I'm sorry. I'll be OK.' Yikes. I must be growing up and maturing or something.

Grandma smiles approvingly, and Mum wraps me in a bear hug. Then daddy bear joins in. Fin cracks my ankle with his lightsaber then locks his arms around my knees and dribbles. There's no point fighting it. After all – on the upside, they're taking my little brother with them. The Empire State Building will need steam cleaning, once he's passed his sticky way through it.

Eddie, my big brother, who may not have brushed his hair in the last fortnight, is taking them to the airport. It's not often Mum or Dad consent to get into Eddie's car, not least because it stinks. At least it used to, until Eddie's girlfriend, Susannah, brought deodorant into his life.

'Stick to the rules and you'll be sound,' says Dad. 'As soon as we go, take a look at them.'

I feel my face scrunch with anxiety. Fifty rules! By the time I've finished reading them, they'll be on their flight home. Eddie loads their suitcases. Dad straps Fin into his child seat. Mum gives me a final hug. They pile in.

There's no room for me, obviously. I am the middle child with no clear role in life. I stand close to Grandma hoping she'll put her arm around me. We watch as Eddie backs out of the drive with a look of comic concentration. Mum and Dad wind down their windows and gulp in fresh air. Off they go, down the hill. I imagine Eddie doing a handbrake turn, telling my parents sternly: *You can't leave Ellie behind!* – but of course he doesn't. On Eddie's list of priorities, my welfare is below his compulsion to give tired bees drinks of sugary water, and slightly above his need to wear a shirt and tie – which is never.

'Don't you worry,' says Grandma giving my shoulder a quick squeeze. 'We'll kick up our heels while they're gone.'

We go inside. Herman senses my mood, drops to the floor and puts his sad face on. I sit on the stairs and listen to the house. It's loud with empty noise. It's hard being left behind.

'I'll get a cardigan and we'll take Herman for a walk,' says Grandma.

Herman raises one eyebrow and thumps his tail hopefully.

The 'All Alone and Abandoned' Rule Book is on the edge of the captain's chest. Oh joy. I reach for Herman's lead and accidentally catch the envelope. It falls. Herman jumps, notices his tail and twists, batting the envelope under the chest where fat, hairy spiders have lived in peace for generations. Without even trying, I've removed the quotation marks. Now it really *is* abandoned. I'm devastated, of course, but I'll get over it.

We set off down the hill. Some people may think it's embarrassing to hang out with your grandma. That's probably because they don't have a grandma like mine. I'll clarify. I have two grandmothers. I call the other one, Nanna. Nanna and Gramps lived with us for a while – but they now live in an Assisted Living bungalow in town. It's on a busy street which means there are lots of people for Nanna to disapprove of, which suits her fine. Disapproving is her main hobby.

Grandma, on the other hand, puts a positive spin on almost everything. When a pickled beetroot shot off Fin's plate onto Grandma's new cream skirt she laughed and said, 'Brilliant shot, Fin. Have you been practising?' Grandma kicks off her shoes and paddles in the sea, makes sculptures out of wire and clay, and throws a few interesting shapes on the dance floor when she gets the chance. The best thing Grandma does is listen, especially to me.

The glass doors of the Box Brownie Café are folded back

and there are tables with parasols set out on the promenade. The air is salty and humming with chatter. As we pass, Cadence calls out, 'Ruby!' She swishes her way to us, in time to the juke box music, and pulls out an envelope from her apron pocket.

'From a *gentleman*. He asked if I knew you, gave me this and disappeared without saying another word.' Then, with an air of innocence, 'Is there something you want to tell me, Ruby?'

Grandma takes the pale lavender envelope. Her gnarled hands, which make such beautiful things, shake a little. I am reminded that Grandma is no spring chicken.

'How intriguing,' she says, with a slight wobble in her voice.

'Who's it from?' I demand. Frankly, I don't appreciate the inference that my grandmother has a secret admirer.

Grandma gives a little shrug and tries not to smile. Jeepers! She knows *exactly* who the letter is from, and she's not going to tell me! She's pretty keen to read it too. Cadence goes off to clear tables and I'm left feeling like a spare part. This isn't *quite* how I expected the first day of my summer holiday to go.

I'm not wanted. I leave Grandma at the café and head down the slipway. Herman bounces onto the beach and starts to run. I sprint after him. I'm just getting into my stride when suddenly, Herman stops dead. There's no time to side-step so I launch myself over him and face-plant with a splat.

'You nearly *killed* me!' I say crossly, spitting out sand.

Herman quivers, his nose in the air, not a bit sorry.

Someone laughs. Mortified, I see Bella, the new girl in town, perched on a rock with my arch enemy, Gilby Flynn.

Let me explain. Not so long ago, *I* was the new girl in town. Believe me – *no one* was excited. But Bella – different story. Everyone is falling over themselves to be her friend. She's über-pretty (big cow eyes and long brown hair that actually sparkles – *sickening*) and her father is the new owner of the Little Egret, a posh hotel overlooking the sea. Already she's had sleepovers. Great fun apparently. Meals in the restaurant. Laughing the night away in the jacuzzi. Not that I was invited.

And what can I say about Gilby Flynn? He's TROUBLE. I'd rather have the company of a rock.

I pick myself up and pretend not to notice them. Herman has other ideas. He runs towards Gilby, cocks his leg and pees, kicks sand in Gilby's face, then trots back to me with his nose in the air. Herman is a dog who likes to express his feelings.

At the end of the cove, Herman catches an irresistible scent and he takes off again. We scramble over the rocks and pull ourselves onto the grassy bank in front of the lighthouse. I see Elsie, my best friend, and beside her Cooper and Abigail Jennings are huddled together. Herman wags his tail, then stops and flattens his ears. Something's wrong. Abigail is crying.

'Hi Ellie,' says Elsie, looking embarrassed.

I'm surprised to see them all together. Abigail used to be Cooper's *sort of* girlfriend, until he wised up. Under a microscope, you might find that Abigail has one or two decent qualities, but loyalty isn't one of them – and I know Elsie has her own reasons for not trusting her.

Cooper looks guilty. He shifts awkwardly away from Abigail.

'You may as well know,' mutters Abigail, 'I've got problems at home.'

Her dad, a policeman, isn't the sharpest knife in the drawer. He failed to notice his *own daughter* developing criminal tendencies – but that's another story. *

'My parents are splitting up,' she says, miserably.

That's not what I expected. PC Jennings has always had a lot to say about the importance of family and bringing kids up to follow the rules.

'It might not come to that,' says Elsie, patting Abigail's shoulder.

'Elsie was just telling me how your parents are trying to save their relationship,' Abigail sniffles.

I nearly *choke.* My mum and Elsie's mum are friends and they tell each other loads, but this, MOST DEFINITELY, is misinformation. My parents have had their ups and downs – but they're pretty much fixed now. I am *furious.*

'Elsie says that's why they're going to America,' adds Abigail sounding strangely satisfied.

'You know about *America?*' I splutter. '*I* only found out yesterday!' Elsie has flame coloured hair and now her cheeks are blazing. She knew before *me* and I'm the abandoned kid in this scenario!

'Why are you even *talking* about my family's problems, when you don't even have a dad?' I snap.

Even the seagulls are shocked. One screeches above my head. I look up, and when I look back, Elsie's on her feet. She zaps me with angry eyes then swings round and runs off along the cliff top. A gannet launches itself off the cliff and nosedives into the sea, which is probably what's just happened to my friendship with Elsie.

'How is this *my* fault?' I yell after her.

I look at Cooper, who looks away. Abigail crumples into him and sobs loudly.

Herman's had enough drama. He scrambles down the cliff and I chase after him. Further along the beach, I'm being watched. I hold up my head and try to shape an expression that says, *my day is going so well...*

Bella shouts, 'Hey, you!'

Does she mean *me?* I pretend I don't hear, but Herman has other ideas. He bounds over to Bella who lets out a fearful squeal.

'Herman!' I shout, but he's wearing his cloth ears.

'Will it bite?' cries Bella, using Gilby as a human shield.

Gilby is nervous of dogs and this has always worked to my advantage but, come on – Herman is softer than a baby bunny. Best not share *that* golden nugget.

I go to Herman and clip on his lead.

'It's Ellie? Right?' asks Bella, composing herself. She flicks her hair in a way that sprinkles diamond chips into the atmosphere.

I nod and slide my eyes over Gilby. He sits close to Bella, dangling his feet in a rockpool. Has he had a spray-tan?

Bella looks me up and down. 'I want to pick your

brains,' she says, then adds with heavy sarcasm, 'It won't take long.'

Ouch. That wasn't nice. Gilby sniggers.

'Come up to the hotel,' she says, suddenly friendly. 'We could swim in the pool or work out in the gym.'

I've looked at the Little Egret hotel on the Internet. I would *love* to swim in the pool there. This must be a trick. I give a non-committal shrug.

I look at Gilby's bare feet. If only there were a mutant crab in the pool flexing its pincers.

'How's your leg?' I ask him, coldly.

'Good,' he says, not looking at me.

'All healed up?'

He nods.

'Why? What happened?' asks Bella.

She doesn't know? Gilby broke his leg falling off the stage at school, which is *ironic* because he was trying to break somebody else's bones at the time.*

There is an awkward silence. Herman barks.

'It's an interesting story. Gilby should tell it,' I say.

I walk off thinking, *that was weird.*

Elsie is sitting at a table outside the Box Brownie café. I look for Grandma, but she's gone. It's pretty clear Elsie is still in a dark place. Hostility feels grey and sort of heavy.

'You don't know *anything* about my family,' she hisses as I pass.

'And you don't know anything about *mine*,' I say.

'I *do*.'

'You *don't*.' Already I'm sorry. I've never fallen out with

13

Elsie before.

'Well you have *no* right to say what you said.'

Hang on. Elsie was using my parents as a prime example of a dysfunctional couple. *How could you, Elsie?* I think. *Everything I told you about my parents' problems was strictly **PRIVATE and CONFIDENTIAL.***

My expression might show some RIGHTEOUS INDIGNATION, because Elsie can't look at me. A minute goes by...

'I've been offered a place on a performing arts course. I'll be away all summer,' she announces, coolly.

I absolutely, almost positively, do not know what to say. We're best friends, or at least I thought we were, and this is news to me. Elsie frowns and stares at the horizon. The breeze catches her hair. A seagull cries mournfully. Cue melancholic music – it's a scene from a sad movie.

I can't believe that the things I counted on to make me happy this summer are disappearing. I consider my options. The least humiliating seems to be indifference.

'Well, have a good time,' I hear myself say. I head home with Herman, a lump of lead in my chest for a heart.

Exit Susannah, hello Susie Q

Okay. Things are deteriorating. I mean, *seriously*. I can hear Susannah shouting and it's not friendly. Herman stays at the top of the stairs looking worried, his ears flattened to block the noise. I'm just about to march into the kitchen to tell Eddie to grow up when Susannah storms past me and out of the house. Eddie appears looking like he's been chewed up and spat out.

'Go after her!' I order him, but he just shakes his head and walks away. I rush outside. 'Susannah!' I yell. 'What's he done this time?'

Susannah ignores me, jumps on her moped and speeds away. I can't believe it!

Eddie slumps at the kitchen table. Eliza jumps on his knee and starts to purr, but he gently brushes her off. And then, he puts his head in his hands and sobs. I've never seen my big brother cry before. It's perfectly horrible.

I look around – but there's no Mum or Dad. There's no Grandma. I grab a banana from the bowl. Then I put it back. He's not really an ape and fruit won't fix this.

'What happened?' I ask.

He manages to say, 'It's over.'

'Don't say that,' I say, shaking him a little. 'Go after her and tell her you're sorry.'

Eddie takes a gulp of air. 'Not this time.'

The cracked note in his voice frightens me. He gets up and plods into the workshop, closing the door behind him.

I sit on the garden bench waiting for Grandma to come home. I've tried her mobile three times, but it goes straight to voicemail. I see her car coming up the hill. She swings it into the drive and climbs out.

'Where have you been?' I demand.

'Doing a bit of shopping,' she answers.

I stop in my tracks. There's something different about her. Her movements are freer somehow, as though someone's used an oil can on her creaking joints. She scoops up a bag from the boot.

'I'm going out tonight, so you and Eddie can muddle through, I'm sure.' She breezes past, looking very... *happy*. 'Is everything all right?' she calls over her shoulder, not waiting for an answer.

I don't need a mirror to know how stressed I must look – but Grandma doesn't even notice. She practically skips inside, leaving me standing – abandoned and alone.

I'm in Grandma's sitting room. She drifted out of the house half an hour ago, wearing a new dress, (floral and floaty) pashmina, (duck egg blue) and sling back sandals with kitten heels (nude). Don't panic. I'm no fashionista. I'm just emphasizing that this is not how Grandma normally dresses – it's usually something elasticated and baggy, and her usual footwear fastens with Velcro. I'm not sure I approve. I rely on Grandma to be predictable and **mainly interested in me**. This change hinges on the lavender letter, I'm sure of it. I look around for clues. On

16

the coffee table are books that Grandma has read, and then I see one I've never noticed before: ***Alone But Not Lonely: 100 Rules for Solo Living***. I flick though the pages, which are a bit dog-eared.

Being alone does not have to mean you're lonely.*
Solo life can be a challenge, but one that can be rewarding and successful, so long as you follow simple rules.
There are three basic rules to begin with:
1. Always have a plan. Having something to do wards off loneliness. If you don't have an established routine to follow, devise one. Don't start your day with nothing to do, nowhere to go, and no one to see.
2. Socialise! Get out and about. Be open to new experiences, and remember that you must be friendly in order to make friends.
3. Have at least one trusted person nearby and keep in contact. Everyone needs someone to turn to in an emergency, and it will increase your sense of security.

Why would Grandma even own such a book? After Grandpa died, we came to live with her and now this house is normally stuffed to bursting. I hear Eddie coming up the stairs. I push the book under the coffee table just as he sticks his head around the door.

'What are you doing?' he asks, but he doesn't seem interested in an answer. He looks awful.

My trusted person, at this very moment, is Eddie. He's all I have. I don't even know where Grandma has gone, and as for my parents – it's like they've fallen off the planet. I suddenly feel very, very lonely.

'Have you eaten?' he asks.

'There's nothing to eat in the entire house,' I say. That's not true, but it *feels* true. Grandma's food makes me feel loved and at this moment, no one in this house really loves me, except for Herman, and he can't cook.

Eddie looks alarmed. 'Should I go to the supermarket?'

'Let's get takeaway,' I say.

Eddie parks on the promenade and we eat in the car. I asked for Coca-Cola, but he got me a carton of Ribena, like I was a little kid.

'We'll have vegetables tomorrow,' he says.

'Or we could live on pizza,' I say.

'You need vitamins.'

'I'll eat an orange.'

I don't ask him about Susannah. I don't even feel angry with him. He looks too sad and empty.

'Something's going on with Grandma,' I say. I want to tell Eddie about the lavender letter.

He looks slightly interested but not enough to ask questions. He manages, 'I've a feeling it's going to be you and me, kid.'

That doesn't sound good. Me and Eddie? Eddie and me? Don't tell me Grandma is about to go AWOL* as well?

'Do *you* know what's going on?' I ask him. Eddie was with me when our perfumed grandmother wafted out of the house.

Eddie shrugs, staring out to sea. 'Why would anyone tell *me* what they're planning? I don't matter.'

I get the feeling he's talking about Susannah. I wonder if this time, maybe, it really is over? I don't want to go back to an empty house. Well, it's not exactly empty. Herman will be at his lookout post at the top of the stairs, probably snoring his head off. He doesn't like it when people are sad. He prefers to sleep and wake up when everyone's happy again.

'Let's go and see Susie Q,' I suggest. Susie Q is Eddie's new boat.

We drive along the promenade, turning onto the deserted Coast Road. When we reach Portis Crag where the road forks, we descend over cobbles, bumping our way into the tiny harbour car park. An old man potters with boat work, which is a bit like housework, but more relaxing. I like it here. Time switches to s-l-o-w, and the rest of the world seems to fade away. Susie Q is moored at the end of the jetty. We climb aboard. Eddie picks up a cloth and starts cleaning smudges off the deck. I go inside. It's tidy! Tins and packets of food are neatly stacked on shelves, the little galley gleams, and there are new navy curtains and matching seat cushions printed with white boat wheels. I climb back onto the deck.

'She's lovely,' I say cheerfully, but then we both think of Susannah and our mood goes down.

What did I say two days ago? I'm going to have endless hours of fun and relaxation? This is going to be a stormy summer. Happy holidays. Let the good times roll.

An alternate universe

Grandma flip flops into the kitchen wearing cropped denim jeans and a tunic top printed with bright orange butterflies (scoop neck, cute silver belt) which I might wear, if it came in my size. I'm starting to think someone's stolen Elasticated Waist Grandma, and replaced her with a Marks & Spencer version, all dosed up on vitamins.

'I loaded the dishwasher, Grandma,' I say, to make her notice me and reconsider her responsibilities.

'Great stuff,' she says, dreamily.

Maybe I should take over running the house – and pay the bills as well? I think, but Grandma is not tuning into my thoughts.

It is extremely disappointing to realise I am not the centre of Grandma's universe. Of anyone's universe. This summer is not going to be all about me.

'Where's Herman?' I ask.

'Out with Eddie.'

Excuse me? 'Since when has Eddie gone for morning walks with Herman?'

Grandma smiles. 'There's a first time for everything, Ellie Booton. I do believe the wind of change is blowing,' she says mysteriously.

What on earth does that mean? I am seriously worried.

I jog down the hill and head down the slipway onto the beach. Eddie might be having a nervous breakdown but that's no excuse for stealing my dog. (OK, Herman is technically Grandma's dog, but he's twelve and so am I, which means Herman and I have a special understanding.) I find them by the rocks at the edge of the cove. Herman lays in the sand with his head on Eddie's foot. He thumps his tail a couple of times to greet me, but doesn't lift his head.

'It's beautiful down here,' says Eddie, with no enjoyment in his voice at all. 'I'm going to walk on the beach more often.' He opens his hand. 'I found this.'

'That's unusual,' I say.

He hands it over, no questions asked. I slip it into my pocket.

Later, I log on to Eddie's laptop and check my emails. There's one from Mum.

Hi Ellie

Arrived. Hotel. Exhausted. Fin in crèche full of beans. Fin, that is. Not crèche. Expensive. Don't care. Need sleep.
Good night, morning, whatever. No idea what time it is.
I'm a few hours younger here. Feel ninety.
Love you. Miss you.
Mum xoxo

A different time zone means they really are far away. That doesn't feel good. And then, an email from Jack pops up with an attachment.

Hi Ellie

Catching the train tonight. I'll text Cooper. Hang tomorrow?

Have I told you about Alex? J

I suddenly feel a whole heap better – but not for long. I open the attachment. Jack, who is a bit of a hero in this town, has his arm around a girl. They look perfect together. How very, *very* lovely. I snap the laptop shut. Jack and *Alex*. Cooper and *Abigail*. Elsie and her *performing arts course. Me...*

That settles it. I need a PLAN and a NEW ROUTINE. I need to SOCIALISE. I may need some NEW FRIENDS.

I google Little Egret's website and scribble down the telephone number, then I ring the hotel and ask to speak to Bella. She doesn't rush to answer the phone, that's for sure. *We might become friends,* I think. *I could end up sipping iced drinks by the pool and –*

'Yeah?'

'Oh hi. It's Ellie.'

'Who?'

'Ellie Booton...' Silence. 'Um, you wanted to pick my brains. Remember?'

'Like it was yesterday.'

'It *was* yesterday,' I say, before I process her sarcasm.

'I wasn't serious,' she says.

Oh. That's embarrassing. There's an awkward pause.

'Meet me at the beach café in half an hour,' she commands, and hangs up.

I stare at the phone. Well, *that* was rude.

I sit on the garden bench and look down at the Box Brownie café. It's the last place I want to go. I'm not even sure if Bella will turn up, but eventually she comes into sight at the far end of the promenade.

I saunter down the hill, pacing myself so she gets there first. She parks herself under a parasol, texting like there's no tomorrow. Without looking up she says, 'What's going on with you and Gilby?'

I'm thinking, *what?* – when Cadence breezes by to take our order.

'Thanks for persuading Elsie to go, Ellie,' says Cadence, warmly.

Am I in an alternate universe? Did I fall and bang my head?

'You're welcome,' I say, doubtfully. 'She's gone then?'

'This morning.' Cadence looks at Bella and smiles. 'My daughter was offered a place on a prestigious performing arts course. It's a great opportunity for her.'

'How proud you must be,' says Bella, rudely.

Bella's sarcasm isn't lost on Cadence who frowns and flicks the table with her cloth. Then Bella digs her hands into her pockets, shrugs and says, 'I don't have any money.'

I've been raised to be responsive and polite, which is, occasionally, a pain in the butt. 'Don't worry,' I say. 'I'll pay.'

Bella orders cappuccino and a biscotti; I order cola. My teeth can rot. It's my parents' fault for leaving me without adequate supervision.

Bella is, apparently, easily distracted. She reads a text,

laughs, and texts a reply while I sit, feeling like a spare part. When people have bad manners, it makes you think all sorts of negative things about them. Finally, she slips her phone into her moneyless pocket, gives me an anguished look and says, 'Did you know the Little Egret is haunted?'

I'm not withholding information – I'll account for my conversation with Bella soon, I promise.

I sprint along the track, past the lighthouse, and climb over the stile at the far side of the cornfield. I run across Portis Crag for a short way, cross the Coast Road, then join the footpath onto Curly Lane, heading up to Hope Hill where Juna lives. Juna knows what it's like to feel trapped in a dark tunnel. It's been a strange day and I need to see some light.

As I pass one of the cottages, there's movement. I'm surprised to see Juna huddled on the doorstep cradling a small, scruffy dog. I slip through the garden gate. The dog struggles in Juna's arms and the air seems to shimmer with heat and uncertainty.

'Am I glad to see you!' says Juna, relieved. She reaches out and grasps my hand.

'What's going on?' I perch on the step beside her.

'I walk Tilly for Mrs Williams. When I got here, there was an ambulance and they've taken her away. Now Tilly's all by herself.'

I reach out to stroke Tilly, who is too upset to respond. *Another creature with abandonment issues,* I think.

'Can you look after her until Mrs Williams gets home?'

I ask.

Juna barely shakes her head. Reading between the lines, it's pretty obvious that money's tight in Juna's family. Let's face it – a dog is another mouth to feed.

'Could a neighbour take her?' I ask.

'People came out to see what was going on, then they all walked off. No one seems to care,' says Juna.

'We could ask Eddie what we should do,' I suggest.

'Eddie?' says Juna. I guess it's obvious that Eddie's not a natural leader. 'Sorry, Ellie,' she adds. 'I like Eddie. He's very nice.'

'Well, he's more sad than nice,' I say. 'Susannah's dumped him.'

'Oh no. Poor Eddie,' says Juna.

I bullet point what's happened over the weekend:

- Mum and Dad's trip to America.
- How I came across Abigail cosying up to Cooper on the cliff top.

'I don't understand *that,*' says Juna. *'Abigail?* What was he *thinking?'*

- And how Elsie suddenly decided to go on a performing arts course.

'I said something to Elsie–' I really don't want to revisit that memory. 'Anyway, for whatever reason, she's gone,' I say, feeling sad and guilty.

I have Herman's lead in my pocket. I clip it on Tilly's collar, but she's unwilling to leave her home. For a small dog, she's *big* on determination. Juna struggles with her resistance, then picks her up. Out of nowhere, a gust of wind practically blows us out of the garden and slams the gate behind us.

The wind of change. I don't like it.

Growing list of people who have blown away...

Mum, Dad, Fin, Susannah, Elsie. And now, Mrs Williams. Gone. Oh, and Cooper, who's cosying up with Abigail and acting like an ex-friend.

'And Grandma...' I say, pausing for dramatic effect. 'I think she has a *boyfriend*.' Juna's look says it all. 'I know. Pretty weird, huh?'

Let's face it. An abandonment theme is definitely taking shape.

We reach home, exhausted. It's been difficult getting Tilly this far. I open the door and Herman hurtles down the stairs. He skids to a stop, smelling fear. Tilly quivers in Juna's arms. Herman searches the air for clues: human anxiety and Tilly's raw confusion – but there's no threat. He wags his tail, cautiously. *There's nothing to be frightened of. I'll be your friend. Just don't steal my biscuits, that's all I ask.*

We find Eddie in the workshop. His concentration reminds me of Grandma when she works. He presses clay onto the wire frame of a wide-winged gannet. It's taking shape and it's... beautiful. I feel a stab of something in my chest. I think it might be pride?

Eddie stops and lets Tilly sniff his hand. He doesn't ask questions – he just sits quietly and lets us explain.

'What should we do?' I ask, finally.

26

'She's stressed,' says Eddie. 'Give her some water and offer her something to eat.'

'Poor Tilly,' says Juna. 'It must be awful when someone you love suddenly leaves, and you don't understand why.'

Eddie gulps. We look at one another and share a thought about Susannah.

'So, can we look after her?' I ask.

'Sure,' says Eddie, simply.

I'll be honest. I feel intimidated with the responsibility of looking after another lost soul. I have my hands full with Eddie.

'Tilly would settle if Juna stayed,' I say.

'Whatever works,' says Eddie.

I can't quite believe how accommodating my token adult is. I look at Juna, appealingly.

'That would be nice,' she says, pleased.

'Clear it first. Ask Grandma to phone Juna's mum to make sure it's OK,' says Eddie. He thinks for a moment then says, 'We should let Mrs Williams know that Tilly's safe. I'll phone the hospital.'

'Thanks, Eddie.' For some reason, I wrap my arms around Eddie's neck and snuggle my face in his tangled hair. For a moment, I'm caught in his sense of loss – a powerful current dragging him down. It's scary to realise that we don't always have control over what happens to us.

Grandma appears from another shopping trip (new sunglasses, straw hat and a jar of anti-wrinkle cream for mature skin). I tell her about Mrs Williams.

'Oh dear. Poor Jenny. I'll visit her in hospital,' says Grandma, sounding concerned.

Then Juna comes into the kitchen with Tilly in her arms and I explain our plan to look after her, hopeful that Grandma will be supportive.

'Jenny will be relieved Tilly's safe, I'm sure. Of course, you're welcome to stay, Juna. You're Tilly's trusted person. It will increase her sense of security to have you close by.'

Hang on. Isn't that advice from *Alone But Not Lonely: 100 Rules for Solo Living?* Are all Grandma's nuggets of wisdom stolen from books?

Grandma telephones Juna's mum, and it's all fixed. Honestly – calm, practical adults are worth their weight in gold. Let's face it – there aren't that many of them.

Later, when we've collected an overnight bag from Juna's, we go up to my bedroom to organise ourselves. We make a bed for Tilly on the floor beside the bottom bunk where Juna will sleep.

I find Grandma in her sitting room, perched on her window seat in the evening sun, painting her toenails *Sunset Gold.*

'Grandma,' I say. 'What can we do to help Tilly? She's had a drink, but she won't eat. She looks so lonely.'

'Lonely, but not alone,' says Grandma softly. 'I *so* get that.'

'You're not lonely Grandma,' I say. 'You have me.'

'True,' says Grandma.

Then I notice that Grandma is looking rather snazzy. Another new skirt (pleated and peachy) and a cream blouse (with see-through sleeves).

'Are you going out, Grandma?' I ask. I detect disapproval in my voice.

Grandma hesitates. 'I'm meeting a friend for dinner.'

'Oh,' I say. 'Who is your friend?'

She's not in the mood to answer questions.

'Eddie will look after you,' she says, firmly. 'There's food in the fridge and you know how to eat sensibly, and what *not* to watch on TV, and where *not* to go on the Internet, and *when* to go to bed. Mind you, you're on holiday, so I don't suppose it matters too much – bedtime I mean. Rules apply to the other stuff, as you are well aware.' She peers at me over her glasses.

'Where are you going?' I ask crossly, because she's leaving me, and I'm entitled to feel abandoned.

'The Little Egret.'

Hang on... *Dinner at the Little Egret?* The *haunted* Little Egret? I adjust my attitude. This might be interesting.

'When you get home, I want to know *every* last detail.'

'Really?' says Grandma, surprised.

'Yes. And Grandma, don't let anyone or *anything* creep up behind you.' I give Grandma a meaningful look. Grandma looks a bit shocked. I mean, there was a *reason* why I ran along Portis Crag to find Juna.

Truth, lies and manipulation

Juna is a good listener. She doesn't over-react and she's practical. She's what my mum would call, *self-contained.* I guess she's had to rely on herself an awful lot.

We sit on the window seat in my bedroom and watch the sun sink into the sea. Tilly is panting, a sure sign of stress. Meanwhile, my stress levels have gone up a few notches as I spill the beans to Juna.

Stress factors:

* I have no idea how to read Bella. She seems friendly, but then she's sarcastic and edgy.

* **She's friends with Gilby.**

* I don't think Bella's lying, but she's weird. She told me a creepy story and I think I believed her.

* Did I mention – **she's friends with Gilby.**

* Why has Bella chosen me to confide in? She doesn't even know me – and what has Gilby said about me?

Considering all of the above, I am a bit freaked out, not least because –

SHE'S FRIENDS WITH GILBY!

'So, she heard something go bump in the night?' asks Juna, unimpressed.

'In the early hours of this morning. She heard movement in the room above hers.'

'Rats.' says Juna. 'We had them in the loft once.'

'It's not a loft,' I say. 'It's a guest bedroom but it wasn't occupied. Anyway, how can there be rats running around? It's a *hotel.*'

'They're on holiday?' suggests Juna.

We snigger. 'This morning she checked the room and the door number was different.'

'I don't understand,' says Juna.

'It had somehow changed from twenty-nine to twenty-six. That's definitely spooky.'

Herman twitches in his sleep and snores loudly. His stress levels are set to zero. Lucky dog.

Grandma pops her head around the door, making us jump.

'Eddie's made vegan lasagne. He's used the oven and the kitchen isn't on fire,' she says, cheerfully.

'Grandma's going to the Little Egret for dinner,' I say to Juna, nudging her. Then I have a thought. 'Is your friend staying there?' I ask.

'He is,' says Grandma.

Ha! I knew it! She's having dinner with Lavender Letter Man.

'What's his room number?'

Grandma's shocked for some reason. 'Ellie Booton, I'm sure I don't know,' she says.

'Will you find out tonight?' I ask. I'm wondering if his

31

room is anywhere near the spooky room.

'I most certainly will *not!*' she says huffily.

Honestly, I don't understand grown-ups sometimes. They want to know *where* you are, *what* you're doing, *who* you're with and *how* long you'll be. I ask Grandma a simple question and it's like I've asked her to breach the Official Secrets Act or something.

Grandma drives off and Juna and I take Herman and Tilly into the garden. Tilly sniffs around cautiously and pees. For anyone with knowledge of dogs, this is a good sign and Juna and I smile at one another, proudly.

On the promenade, in the distance, I see Cooper.

'How can you tell that's him?' asks Juna.

I recognise his walk. I feel pain. When he had his arm around Abigail, he couldn't look at me. I thought we were friends.

'Won't be a minute.' I say. I go inside. Eddie's in the kitchen, tossing knives and forks on the table.

'Is there enough to feed one more?' I ask.

'Human or dog?' asks Eddie.

'Human,' I say.

'Sure,' says Eddie.

I notice Eddie's fingernails are clean – for quite a few years, they weren't. And even though his heart is breaking, he's cooked.

I swallow. 'Thanks Eddie.'

I run down the hill. When I reach the promenade, Cooper has already turned down the slipway onto the beach and is doubling back, hands in pockets, head down.

Catching up, I tap his shoulder, making him jump. We stand and look at one another. He's aimless and sad. I see a boy who struggles to fit in.

'Lasagne?'

His expression brightens. 'Grandma's?'

'Eddie's.'

He thinks for a moment. 'I'll risk it.'

Over dinner, I retell the story of the haunted Little Egret and room number twenty-nine.

'Someone's messing about,' says Eddie.

'How are the numbers fixed to the door? Are they screwed on?' asks Cooper.

'No idea,' I say.

'Well if they're screwed on, all you'd have to do is take the nine off, flip it, and fix it back on.'

I love that about Cooper. He's so logical.

'But why would someone do that?'

Cooper shrugs. 'Maybe it was a mistake. Maybe she's attention seeking?'

'What do you mean? She's making it up?' asks Juna.

'It's not unknown,' says Cooper, with a hint of bitterness.

The air is suddenly static.

Cooper takes a deep breath. 'I saw Abigail's parents this morning looking as normal as they can look for the oddest couple in town. Cop Jennings was practically carrying a copy of Marriage Vows Weekly.'

'Maybe they've sorted out their problems?' I say.

'Or maybe Abigail's trying to provoke a reaction by

spinning a story,' snorts Cooper.

'Well, in that case, Abigail's caused a heap of trouble between me and Elsie.' I give a brief outline of Elsie's sudden departure. 'We've never fallen out before and now she's gone for the summer.'

Eddie's mood is suddenly flat. Susannah might be gone forever.

'Maybe Bella's trying to get a reaction too,' says Juna.

'Don't let this new girl manipulate you, Ellie,' says Eddie, frowning. 'She sounds a bit strange.'

What I know about manipulation:

* Manipulation is like a mind game. The manipulator wants to influence or control someone's thoughts and actions.
* I'm not sure manipulation is easy. It probably takes imagination, planning and persistence. Come to think of it, so does persuasion, though persuasion seems more artful, open and honest. Persuasion also requires a bit of charm and negotiation.
* I don't like the idea of being manipulated. I guess I'm open to persuasion.
* Mum says Jane Austen* wrote a book called Persuasion, and it's a must-read at some point in my life.

Let's backtrack. Abigail seemed genuinely upset. Why would she lie about her parents' relationship? As for Bella,

I don't know her but there's a warning light flashing in my head.

'Bella wants me to visit the Little Egret,' I say. 'Why would she want attention from *me?* It doesn't make sense.'

'Why wouldn't she?' asks Cooper, helping himself to more garlic bread. 'Why wouldn't anyone?'

Juna swallows. 'I guess people reach out in different ways.'

It's true that, in the past, Juna found it hard to communicate her worries. That's one thing Juna, Cooper and I have in common. And another – Gilby. I've already told you that he made our lives a misery. He never apologised and now, if he did, it would be **too little, too late.**

The air hangs heavy.

'If you go to the Little Egret – we all go,' says Cooper, fixing me with steady eyes.

Juna agrees.

'OK,' I say. 'On one condition. We include Abigail. Maybe she just wants to be friends?'

'Addendum,' says Eddie, firmly. 'Clear *everything* with me first.'

Juna widens her eyes and takes a sip of Cherry Good.

Eddie's in *loco parentis.** How strange is that?

Just before bed, I check my email. No one loves me. Slight exaggeration, but it would have been nice to get a message from Mum. Whenever she goes away, I miss her. Even when she's home, she's sometimes not 'here' if you know what I mean. Actually, I hope you *don't* know what I mean. A depressed parent is a big deal. My heart is starting to ache... Falling out with Elsie, my best friend, is a pretty horrible experience. I take a deep breath and start an email:

Hi Elsie
Are you having fun? What are you up to?

I stare at the screen for a couple of minutes. I delete it and start again...

Hi Elsie
I said a silly thing yesterday.

Hi Elsie
I said a stupid thing yesterday and I'm sorry. I hope you're OK. I hope you'll have lots of fun.

Hi Elsie
I said a stupid thing yesterday and I'm sorry. Please forgive me. I hope you're OK. I'm going to miss you this summer, but I hope you'll have lots of fun. Let me know how you're doing.
Lots of love, Ellie xxx

PS. You're going to be famous one day, so pay attention in class. No slacking! ☺

I climb the stairs to my bedroom. Tilly is curled up next to Juna's bunk, quietly dealing with her anxiety. Herman is at his lookout post at the top of the stairs. Grandma is still out, and he'll stay there until she gets home. Things won't be normal for Herman until my parents and Fin return from America. It's going to be a long summer for him.

I'm grateful Juna's here. I climb on the top bunk and drop my arm over the side. Juna holds my hand for a moment and gives it a gentle shake.

Whatever is going to happen – we're in this together.

Seeing things NOT in the best light

It's early. We're in the kitchen eating breakfast. The French doors are open and the summery fragrance of honeysuckle wafts in from the garden. Birds tweet. There's a sense of peace in the house – then the phone rings.

Eddie answers it and says, 'Sure. Just a minute.'

He covers the mouthpiece and whispers, 'It's Bella.'

I take the phone. Bella launches into a tirade. It's a lot to take in and I wonder if I've reached that age when I need to start the day with a mug of strong coffee.

She didn't sleep well. There were strange noises in the night. Had she told me that the door number had changed? Did I believe her? Things had disappeared! Had I any idea how scary it was? Anyway, she doesn't care what I think – the hotel is haunted!

I listen, patiently. There's no gap for me to speak. Then Bella asks if I will go to the hotel, and I know there's no way I'd want to go by myself. Explaining my *entourage* might be a bit tricky though. I don't think she rated me as a girl with a life and friends.

Bella says, 'Who's he?' when I mention Cooper. 'That *mousey* girl?' when I tell her Juna is staying with me. When I explain Tilly she says, rudely, 'What are you? An animal shelter?'

'If you'd like me to visit, my friends will come too. And Tilly – she can't be left on her own – it wouldn't be fair.'

There's silence, then she says, 'Does the dog know how to behave?'

I look at Tilly, a small, sad scrap with impeccable manners.

'We *all* know how to behave,' I say.

'Come up!' snaps Bella and puts the phone down.

What does *that* mean? This very *minute?*

Eddie texts Cooper to ask him to meet Juna and me in half an hour. We might as well get it over with.

At the junction of Curly Lane, we see Cooper – and *very* close by, Abigail. Cooper has texted her to join us – and I only have myself to blame.

I wave, but Abigail is impassive. She's wearing sunglasses, which makes her impossible to read. Cooper smiles but looks distinctly uncomfortable. This is going to be an exercise in maturity, and I need to be careful. I am not well-practised.

'So, Bella thinks the hotel is haunted? What is she? *C-razy?* sneers Abigail.

Oh. Good start. *Attitude.*

'Let's keep an open mind,' I say. 'What's important is that she's reached out.' Good grief. I sound like my mum! I notice Cooper backs off from Abigail as he strides along, wedging himself between me and the prickly hawthorn hedge.

We retrace our steps, cross the road and turn right, along Portis Crag and the Coast Road. Abigail's wearing flip-flops, so we have to go at her pace. The crosswind pummels us. It'd be a great day for sailing. When we pass the shortcut to Hope Hill, Tilly pulls on her lead and whimpers.

'Sorry Tilly,' says Juna. 'You can't go home yet. Your mum's still in hospital.'

'You're talking to a dumb dog?' says Abigail, scornfully.

'Dogs aren't dumb,' replies Juna, firmly. Her confidence has definitely grown.

'All they want is some idiot who will feed them.'

Well, that didn't take long. It's official. I don't like her.

We turn into the Little Egret's drive. I've never walked up here before and it's a steep, twisting climb. I turn back to look at the view. At the far edge of the cove, the windows of the Box Brownie café wink in the morning sun. The track to the lighthouse cuts through the cornfield and forks to join Portis Crag, a rocky patch of land running from the cliff edge to the Coast Road. The narrow harbour road cuts across the crag and disappears, winding down to the harbour where Eddie's boat is moored. I can just make out Susie Q bobbing in the bluest sea, spangled with chips of pure light. It's a cheerful scene. I take a deep breath of salty air. I need to carry this frame of mind forward.

I catch up and touch Juna's shoulder. She smiles. At the top of the drive the hotel weathervane comes into view: a golden little egret, though little egrets are white in reality, its wings unfurled as though in flight. And then, we're on the level. The first thing I notice is Jack. Then I see what *he* sees. We all do.

We stand and look – *dumbfounded*. I've never used that word in my journal before – but it's the right word, because no one speaks. We're just too... *astonished*. Despite the sun, I shiver.

The hotel sign has been defaced. The 3-D letters of LITTLE have been obliterated with red paint. At least I hope it's paint. The word, 'BITTER' is roughly painted on the wall above them, and "R" is daubed in front of EGRET. The hotel is licensed for weddings, but only pessimists would marry at a venue called BITTER REGRET. Let's face it – they'd be doomed. Paint has dribbled down the wall. The stains on the ground look like splashes of blood.

Jack walks over to us. 'Weird, huh?'

'What are *you* doing here?' I ask him.

'Cooper texted me.'

'I thought we might need some backup,' says Cooper.

Looking at the state of the hotel – I would say, we do. Definitely.

Abigail doesn't know Jack, but already she's more interested in him than anything else.

We look up in silence. This vandalism is not the work of a ghost, unless, of course, the ghost had a pot of paint and a ladder. There are marks in the gravel where it was dragged into place.

On the first floor a curtain twitches and Bella appears, still in her PJs. She draws back one curtain, opens the window and pokes her head out, apparently unaware of the altered signage just below her.

'You're early!' she yells in a – let's be real – *accusatory* tone. She glares at me, notices Jack, adjusts her attitude

41

and flashes a perfect smile.

A moment of sadness creeps into my heart. I know, in the whole of my life, I will never look like her. Jack, to his credit, does not seem distracted. To be honest, our privileged point of view feels very awkward.

The letters for *LITTLE,* once satin-black, look like they've been through a bloody massacre. Jack points to the sign below Bella's balcony. It takes her a moment to refocus her attention. She leans over and looks down. Her eyes pop out on stalks. Um, maybe not such a good look. She disappears and we hear her scream: 'DAAAAAAD!'

We've been herded into the conservatory by a nervous young woman wearing a scarlet uniform. We perch between potted palms on creaky basket chairs, not speaking. Bella's dad is obviously shocked. He paces outside, barking angrily into his smartphone.

'Not tomorrow! **TODAY!** I want you here by nine, not a minute later. Matt white for the wall, satin black for the sign. Got it? This has to be put right, *immediately!'*

He's not a patient man, that's for sure. He's not a looker either, so Bella's lucky that her dad's DNA managed to scramble her face into something so decent. He marches in and says, **'RIGHT!** Which one of you is *responsible* for this **DISGUSTING** act of **VANDALISM?'**

Don't jump to conclusions, but this isn't a new experience for me. Abigail's dad, PC Jennings, once accused Eddie of vandalism – but that's *another* story.*

The cheek of it! I find myself on my feet, squaring up to him.

42

'*Eine* minute bitte!' I snap, not quite sure why I'm speaking German.

'Excuse me?' says Bella's dad, swivelling his head like a startled parrot.

'Just one *minute*,' I say. 'We are *not* responsible for *that!*' I flip my hand indicating the hotel sign. 'We're here because your *daughter* invited us, and the first thing we saw was your *scary* sign – which, frankly, is not what we expected to see.'

It's a good job my parents are on a different continent. I'd be grounded for a year if they could hear me now. On the other hand, Grandma might be cheering.

Cooper stands beside me. 'Search our pockets for tins of paint if you like,' he says, cheekily.

'It happened before any of us got here,' says Jack. 'I was here first and the paint was dry.'

'And *how* would you know that?' snaps Bella's dad.

'I touched the wall where it had splashed,' says Jack, with a touch of attitude.

'Don't use that condescending tone with me!'

'*Sorry.* I *really* didn't *mean* to,' says Jack, sounding even more condescending.

Tilly moves forward and strains on her lead. She's chosen a side. Good for her.

'And *what* is a dog doing here? Dogs have fleas! *Mio Dio!* Where's Liam?' he splutters, and marches out.

For the record, Tilly does not have fleas. We exchange glances. Minutes tick by and it's all rather uncomfortable. Then things start to happen.

Bella makes an entrance. I'm briefly mesmerized:

43

where did she get those *shoes?* What *shampoo* does she use? But then we all swivel towards the sound of a car jetting up the drive. I recognise it – a black BMW – which belongs to Gilby Flynn's dad.

'Liam,' announces Bella.

True enough, *Liam* Flynn jumps out of the car and a moment later, out hops Gilby. They stare at the defaced sign looking horrified. Liam inspects the drag-marks in the gravel, then whips out his smartphone and starts taking pictures. He runs his hand over the wall to test the dryness of the paint dribbles, (more photographs) and loudly states the obvious, that the hotel has been subjected to *blatant and serious vandalism.*

'Bitter regret? Is that a *threat?'* shouts Liam, bitterly.

'Keep it down,' orders Mr Vittori. 'We need to be discreet.'

'Of course,' says Liam. He shakes his head and adds, regretfully, how potentially damaging this could be to the hotel's reputation. A few guests leave the hotel and head for the car park. Most don't look back, but those who do are pounced on and told, *'Strictly no photographs! Thank you!'* by a no-nonsense Liam. He puts a kindly arm around Bella's traumatized dad and steers him into the reception area of the hotel.

'Liam will know what to do,' breathes Bella.

'Is he a detective?' asks Juna.

'He's our PR consultant.' Bella stares at us then snaps, 'PR? Public relations? Oh, for goodness sake. He controls what people *think!'*

Definition of 'PR consultant'

Someone who manages information between a person, a business, or an organisation and the general public in a way to present *said* person, business or organisation in the **best light.**

I can tell you one thing: no one, especially Gilby Flynn's dad, can control what *I* think.

Bella slips out to see Gilby, who looks – what's the word? – *ecstatic* – to see her. Holy moly, is it *obvious* he has a MAJOR CRUSH. Bella says something to Gilby. He looks up, sees us, and crashes his smile. We all have issues with Gilby. Let's just say, when someone (Gilby) has wilfully hurt people (*lots* of people) and has NEVER apologised – well, it's hard to forgive and forget, and I guess he knows that's how we feel.

Bella heads back to the conservatory. Gilby hesitates then skulks after his dad. Good. I don't want him in the same space as me.

'Oh,' says Bella, thinking he was right behind her. 'What happened to Gilby?'

It's awkward when you know stuff that another person doesn't, especially if it's *bad* stuff.

'I don't think he could face us,' I say.

'Meaning?' asks Bella.

I'm not sure what to say.

'Tell me!' she demands.

'Another time,' says Jack, firmly, then adds, 'It's complicated.'

Surprisingly, Bella backs down. She studies Jack for a

moment then says, 'Come with me.'

We *all* follow her. We climb four flights of a wide staircase to the second floor, and head down a carpeted corridor that swallows the sound of our footsteps, past doors numbered twenty-six, twenty-seven, twenty-eight, and stop at the door of room number... twenty-six.

'Room twenty-nine,' says Bella. 'except the number changed in the night.'

The number *is* screwed to the door. Cooper and I exchange looks.

'Last night, I set a trap.'

The corridor is eerily quiet. I guess a part of me wants there to be a ghost behind that door.

It creaks and opens inward a fraction. I glance at Bella who seems genuinely frightened. A shiver snakes down my spine.

Jack steps forward and gives the door a hefty push. There's contact and an anguished cry, then a body launches itself at Bella, who lets out a piercing scream. I scream too, and I'm not the only one.

'You little *****!' yells Bella.

I won't write down what she calls him, but I wouldn't get away with language like that at home. The (bleep) is, apparently, Bella's younger brother, Eden. He runs down the corridor, howling.

If Liam Flynn's job is to present the hotel in its best light, he'll need to crank up the wattage and add some floodlights.

'Wait till I tell Dad, *moron*,' shouts Bella.

'Ugly troll!' yells Eden.

Cooper calmly takes a Leatherman from his pocket, unscrews the 6, flips it, and screws it back.

'Room twenty-nine. Fixed,' he says.

'Mystery solved. Blame the moronic kid,' says Jack, wryly.

I can't help wondering if it's really that simple.

Things to bitterly regret

Juna's mum says she can stay at my house – at least while Mrs Williams is in hospital. I never expected to become friends with Juna – but I can't tell you how glad I am that she's here with me now.

Eddie seems obsessed with fruit and vegetables and making sure that Juna and I have vitamins and enough sleep. Oh, and sunblock, factor gazillion, I think. He's more protective than my actual parents and is definitely in *loco parentis*, because Grandma is unofficially 'on holiday'. She practically skips out of the house in a morning, calling over her shoulder that her mobile is charged and switched on in case of emergency. I'm used to Grandma being there for me when I have no emergencies to report. I am the apple of Grandma's eye. I don't know what she's playing at.

Grandma isn't the only puzzle. I'm now convinced that Abigail has tried to mislead us. There have been numerous sightings of her parents, PC and Mrs Jennings, displaying their default *happy marriage* behaviour. PC Jennings carries the shopping and automatically opens doors for Mrs Jennings, who waltzes through, then falls half a step behind him due to her slightly slower factory setting.

'What's the plan today?' asks Eddie over breakfast.

'Bella's dad invited us to swim in the pool, probably to make up for calling us criminals.'

'Well, keep hydrated,' says Eddie, 'and wear plenty of sunblock.' Eddie puts the breakfast pots in the dishwasher and goes into the workshop. He reappears briefly and says, 'And take an orange or an apple. You need vitamins.'

'I've never eaten so much flippin' fruit,' I mutter to Juna, feeling the pressure.

'He's looking out for us,' says Juna. 'It's not a bad thing.'

It's true. I don't know how it's happened, but Eddie is now someone I feel safe with. He's thinking ahead to keep our lives on track. I thought we had run out of Cherry Good – but we hadn't – and he gave me a bamboo toothbrush. I didn't even know I needed one. He drives to the supermarket and stocks up the freezer. He cooks. Just when I discover my brother *isn't* a limp lettuce, (as Dad once called him) Susannah does a runner. It hurts to think that Susannah doesn't want Eddie, or me, in her life anymore.

The white board on the kitchen wall is blank. Dad scribbled thoughts and questions on it every day. I pick up the marker and write:

If people were plants, what would they be?

'Susannah would be a runner bean,' I say.

'I'd be a turnip,' says Juna.

'You would not! You'd be something bright and cheery. A daisy. No, a daffodil.'

'Bella would be an exotic flower,' says Juna.

'An orchid – definitely. Gilby would be a Venus fly trap

49

– always out to zap somebody.'

We decide Grandma would be a rose, fragrant and plump, even though her petals are drooping. Eddie would be some sort of fruit bush – probably raspberry – all tangled, but still producing something colourful and good.

'I would be a... radish,' I say, 'because not everybody wants them in their salad.'

'I like radishes,' says Juna. 'They're my favourite.'

Oh, before I forget, if you were wondering what Bella's trap was, she had placed something on the bedside table, and it had *disappeared*. We'd already decided that Eden was responsible and had probably unscrewed the 9 and flipped it, just like Jack said. Who knows why?

The thing that doesn't quite make sense though, is the BITTER REGRET attack. I mean, that type of vandalism is serious stuff.

BITTER

Adjective: feeling hurt, resentful or angry in response to a bad experience.

REGRET

Noun: A feeling of disappointment, sadness or repentance over something one has done, or failed to do.

A bitter regret seems to be a confused mix of angry-sad feelings over something that might or might not have happened. I don't get it. Anyway, I just can't see Eden dangling from a ladder in the middle of the night sloshing paint around. It's sinister. So, if Eden didn't do it – who did?

Juna and I set off with Tilly and Herman. Seagulls wheel overhead in a cloudless sky. It's a perfect day. I wonder what my parents and Fin are doing – and if Elsie is enjoying her course. It's strange that everyone has scattered to the winds and I've slipped into another life.

We reach Portis Crag. Susie Q bobs distantly at the end of the jetty. Further along the Coast Road, we turn into the Little Egret's drive and the hotel comes into sight. Any sign of yesterday's vandalism has gone. The letters of Little Egret have been restored to their satin-black finish and stand bold against the dazzling white wall. Across the garden, the swimming pool ripples gently. Abigail huddles with Jack under a parasol. I wave at Cooper who sits on the side, dangling his feet in the water. Bella appears through the rose garden with her dad. He gives a polite cough.

'Hello,' beams Mr. Vittori, flashing a smile that would make his dentist proud. 'I hope you'll enjoy our *beautiful* pool. It's a small way to thank you for being, er, discreet.'

'Have the police found out who did it?' asks Jack, reasonably.

Mr. Vittori hesitates. 'Let's not worry about that.' He laughs awkwardly. 'It was *regretful* – but it's over now and we need to move on. So, please have fun and behave yourselves, er... children.'

Technically, we are still 'children' but at our ages we don't need to be told to 'behave'. I squirm and somehow lose my grip on Herman's lead. He breaks free – *'No!'* – and thunders towards the pool. I know exactly what's going to happen. It's a Labrador thing – they love water almost as much as food. In s-l-o-w motion, Herman launches himself in a bid to displace as much water as he possibly can. He is devilishly effective. Mr. Vittori is *drenched*. Now, *that's* cause for *bitter regret*. To make matters worse, Herman picks up a scent. He paddles frantically to the shallow end, scrambles out of the pool, gives a disgusting cough, and charges off.

'Portia!' screams Bella. 'Don't let your dog hurt her!'

I am already in hot pursuit. 'Who's Portia?' I call over my shoulder.

'My cat, stupid!' shouts Bella.

'He won't,' I shout, running after Herman. 'He's a good dog.' *Oh, the irony. Oh, the shame.*

I race around the corner and barrel over Herman, who has suddenly put the brakes on. A black cat blinks lazily from the top of a wall. She is clearly disgusted and completely *over* it. It's hard to believe Herman was chasing her. He's not a fan of cats. They usually humiliate him.

How to apologise to an indignant cat, learned from bitter experience.

    * Cats don't tolerate insincerity, so mean what
    you say.
    * Don't patronise - just give the facts.
    * Don't expect to be forgiven. Remember, cats
    have their own rules.

'I'm sorry, Portia,' I say. 'Herman shouldn't have done that. He's impulsive and immature.' *Good grief. Have I turned into my dad?*

I eyeball Herman who squints, unable to look at me, his body quivering with shame.

I look around to see Eden leaning against the wall. I expect him to say something obnoxious, but instead he says, 'My dad will give you a lecture. Just ignore him.'

He pats Herman kindly and wanders off. I pick up Herman's lead and, hangdog, we trudge back to the pool.

'People who can't control dogs shouldn't have them,' announces Mr Vittori, projecting his voice to reach me.

'He's normally a good dog,' I say.

'But not today,' observes Bella with venom.

'No,' I say quietly. 'Not today. I'm sorry.'

She slinks off in Jack's direction, leaving me to deal with her dad.

Mr Vittori looks over me. 'Dogs are not *sanitary*,' he says coldly. 'Restrain him, or you and your dog will have to leave.'

He checks his smartphone, then strides away.

I feel very small. I perch on the edge of a sun lounger and put my arm around Herman. He's dripping wet, but he's family, and we should stick together.

Juna and Tilly come to sit beside me. 'Don't worry, Ellie,' says Juna. 'We'll paddle in the sea instead.'

She takes out a pad of paper and pencils from her bag and begins to sketch. It's funny how you can expect a day to go one way – and it doesn't. It's not even close.

I take a DECT phone to my bedroom, hold my breath and dial Susannah's mobile. She answers on the eleventh ring.

'Hi Susannah. It's me,' I say.

There's a pause filled with Susannah's disappointment, which crushes me.

'Oh, hi Ellie,' she says.

'What are you doing?'

'Keeping busy,' says Susannah, wearily.

'Me too. We're looking after a little dog called Tilly.' I must mention Eddie – talk him up. 'Eddie's making a *great* job of looking after us.'

'That's good.'

'Um, he's cooking. He gave me a bamboo toothbrush... and we went to see Susie Q.'

'Susie Q?'

'She's lovely. She's Eddie's new–'

'I have to go. Sorry.'

'Susannah?'

And she's gone. I feel so full of emptiness there's no room for hope or happiness in my body. Susannah was always interested in me. But not anymore. I've lost her and so has Eddie. And I still haven't heard from Elsie, who packed our friendship in a suitcase and boarded a train.

Question: Why do people you care for, stop caring?
Answer: I don't know. I really, really don't know.

The phone rings. I think it might be Susannah calling back, but it's Dad.

'Hello Ellie,' he says, sounding like he's not really three thousand miles away.

'What are you doing?' I ask, with a sense of déjà vu.

'Keeping busy,' says Dad.

I can't mess up this opportunity to make a connection. I plunge in.

'I miss you, Dad. I miss Mum and Fin, too. I just think you should know.'

'What have you broken?' asks Dad. 'Is the house still standing? Has there been a fire?'

'I haven't broken anything. And the house is fine,' I say, hurt.

'Has Eddie crashed the car?'

'No! *Jeepers!* I was only saying I miss you.'

'Oh, good,' says Dad, sounding relieved. 'I miss you too, Ellie.' Then, with a bit of mischief in his voice he adds, 'And I'm *sure* you're following the rules.'

Oh, pants. The *'All Alone and Abandoned' Rule Book.* Awkward silence.

'I trust you, Ellie,' says Dad, suddenly serious. 'You're a good kid.'

Oh, BIG grey pants.

'Um, thanks.' I talk up Eddie big style. He deserves it. He's taking his responsibilities seriously – unlike me.

I wander into the hall. A dust bunny drifts across the floor. The flowers that Grandma keeps fresh are wilting. Grandma kept everything on track, but it's almost like she doesn't live here anymore. I know that pesky rule book is under the chest – but I just can't face it.

Fifty rules! They'll crush me.

Things change. It's unclassifiable

Eddie's obsession with fruit now involves putting blueberries on our Rice Krispies. He loads bowls and glasses of orange juice onto a tray and says, 'Follow me.'

The garden table is set for breakfast under an old parasol. The faded stripy cushions from the garden shed are on the chairs. Herman dozes in the shade of Grandma's prized magnolia tree, and Tilly curls up under the willow to quietly think about all she has lost. Eddie brings her a bowl of water and she looks at him with grateful, sad eyes. Eddie is absolutely switched on to looking after us – and that makes me feel better, even though nothing's perfect.

Juna is easy company. She listens. She's constructive and kind. It's strange to think I once sat here, on this garden bench, and thought of reasons why I didn't like her.

'Try texting her,' says Juna, when I tell her Elsie hasn't responded to my email.

I don't have a mobile. Don't laugh. I just don't. Juna doesn't either.

Eddie comes back with a mug of coffee and sits down.

'Can I text Elsie?' I ask him.

He hands me his smartphone which triggers a series of

flashbacks: Eddie handing me toys and books, sharpened pencils, chocolate cherries, money, his old teddy. Eddie's not much of a talker, but like Grandma says, he's definitely a giver.

I hesitate. 'I phoned Susannah,' I tell him.

He's perfectly still and I think he's holding his breath. Now I must tell him that she didn't want to talk to me. My brother exhales and swallows his disappointment.

'Why don't you phone her, Eddie,' I plead. 'You've always managed to patch things up before. Does she know that you love her?'

'She knows,' he says. 'But I have other people to love as well.'

What does *that* mean? He wants a string of girlfriends? He'll be lucky! He tousles my hair, gets up and goes back into the house. He seems older, somehow. Unhappiness ages people.

'What's Susannah like?' asks Juna, in a low tone. They've met, but not enough to know one another.

'She's... perfect,' I say. 'Well, not perfect exactly – but perfect for Eddie.' I sigh and look at Eddie's smartphone.

I text:

Hi Elsie. R U OK? Will ring 2nite 4 a chat. Ellie x ☺

'That's good,' says Juna. 'It's always best to talk things through.'

If you know anything about Juna, who always kept things bottled up, you'll realise just how far she's come.

Grandma drifts into the garden and settles under the parasol.

'Ah, bliss,' she says, kicking off her flip-flops and

slurping a glass of iced lemon tea.

She's carefree but, let's face it – she has responsibilities. I run through a list of what's happened in the last few days, including the BITTER REGRET attack. That should get her attention.

'What a crazy prank,' says Grandma. 'By the time I got there, it had been put right. I saw photos of it though.'

'You were there yesterday?' I ask, shocked.

'I had brunch,' says Grandma primly. 'I saw a dog jump into the swimming pool. He looked *just* like Herman.'

'It *was* Herman!' I fume.

That's why he ran off! He got a whiff of Grandma! I go into questioning mode. I am, after all, her ONLY granddaughter and I know my rights.

'Who showed you photos?' I stare at Grandma. Is she *blushing?*

'Alfred took them on his phone,' says Grandma. She can't help a little smile.

So, his name is *Alfred*, my least favourite name in the *universe*.

'Well, photos weren't allowed, and *Alfred* shouldn't have taken any,' I say. The disapproval in my voice is awful. What is *happening* to me?

This is what I got out of her: she met Alfred last year in a lavender field, on a painting holiday in Tuscany. That's why he wrote to her on lavender paper. Ugh! He's interested in opera, art *and* my grandmother, apparently. Well, Grandma prefers jazz, so that's where this holiday romance, or whatever it is, will fall down.

Grandma looks at me over her glasses and says, 'The

wind of change, Ellie. For goodness sake, relax and go with the flow.'

Yesterday, Juna left her pencil case by the pool so, even though we don't want to, we have to revisit the *Bitter Regret*. We take the short-cut along the track across the cornfield and just as we're climbing over the stile to join the Coast Road by Portis Crag, a black car whizzes past, going much too fast. Brakes squeal and it skids to a stop. Screened by the hedge, we see the passenger door fly open and Gilby Flynn springs out like a ninja. A shouting match follows in savage tones, then Gilby slams the door and the car speeds off, leaving him in a cloud of dust.

Herman's not with us, but Tilly's on high alert: ears pricked, hackles raised. There's no time to think. Instinctively we retreat, scrambling back though the hedge, into the field. We hear Gilby sprint towards us. Juna pushes me into the waist-high corn and leaps after me. We disappear just as Gilby vaults over the stile. He lands awkwardly gives a grunt of pain and falls. Through the stalks I see his feet. He rubs his ankle and winces... then he starts to cry – awful shuddering sobs.

How to react to a totally unexpected and potentially dangerous situation.

Stay calm – if you can.

Think clearly – if you can.

Follow your instincts – and hope they're good ones.

Hearing someone in distress is horrible. Most humans are

programmed to offer help, but Juna grips my wrist and I read her thoughts: *Gilby is not a safe person. Stay hidden!*

Gilby struggles to his feet and limps off. We wait, barely able to breathe, emerging in time to see him disappear towards the cove.

'What was *that?*' Juna whispers.

'Something ugly.'

I've been told off by my parents *plenty,* and I admit, I've been angry with them sometimes – but we would *never* get into an argument like that. I couldn't imagine it.

We get onto the road feeling dazed, and head to the hotel. Workers are busy fixing CCTV cameras to the front of the building. In the car park, Gilby's dad leans against his car, checking his smartphone.

Mr Vittori comes out, all smiles, and calls, 'I took your advice, Liam.' He points to the cameras. They shake hands like best buds, and Liam says something that makes Mr Vittori laugh. No one would guess that Liam Flynn had just had a blazing row with his son.

Keen not to be noticed, we skirt around to the swimming pool and find Bella sitting in a halo of golden light. Sunglasses, lip gloss, iPhone, French manicure. She's so grown-up. How lucky she is to be beautiful.

'At least you didn't bring that other stupid mutt,' she says looking at Tilly with distaste.

There's an awkward silence.

'Hi Bella,' says Juna politely, though there's tension in her voice. Juna finds her pencil case and pops it in her bag.

'We're getting CCTV installed, so if it happens again–' Bella takes off her sunglasses and looks directly at me '–

I'll know who to blame.'

'*It*' is a reference to the attack on the hotel, and I understand from her tone, a nasty inference.

'Any thoughts on the subject, Ellie?' she presses. 'Any *bitter regrets?*'

None. I don't know who attacked the hotel, but I do know one thing – it is not compulsory to play mind games with Bella. I remember Dad's advice on how to respond to tricky people who are trying to goad you.

Keep your dignity -

'I hope you find who was responsible,' I say, evenly.

Show your compassion -

'And I hope your problems sort themselves out.'

And tell the truth – because, as Dad has often told me, a story has no heart without it.

'Herman isn't stupid. He's intelligent, he's good company, and he's kind, unlike some people I know. Goodbye, Bella.'

I see Eden on the other side of the pool. He looks sort of – *lonely*. Tilly trots with us but stops to squat and pee. Then she twists and sniffs her butt. Dogs are big on truth, but dignity – not so much.

I feel Bella's glare stab my back. I tell myself that what she thinks is none of my business and it shouldn't bother me. A parasol shudders in the breeze. The wind of change is blowing, just like Grandma said.

'Why didn't you call me?' asks Cooper. 'I would've gone with you. What if Gilby had turned nasty?'

'We didn't know we would see him,' I say. 'Don't worry.

I don't plan to go there again – and honestly, Gilby wasn't in any shape to bully us. I almost felt sorry for him.'

'You're not serious?' says Cooper, incredulous.

'Sort of,' I say.

Gilby's sobs still play in my head. It's a strange coincidence that the people I like least: Gilby, Abigail and Bella, are miserable souls. I wonder if there's a link between meanness and misery?

On the plus side, I've discovered that Juna and I have a lot in common. She loves animals as much as I do. She draws her thoughts, and I write mine down. She appreciates my brother, and I can see that Eddie's more than his surfer-dude hair and ratty T-shirts. He cares that we eat well, and that's a big deal to Juna who eats a lot of noodles at home – and he keeps track of us, keeping us safe but still feeling free. His heart is broken, like Tilly's – but they're both coping without fuss and doing their best. It's funny how the sad, brave eyes of a dog can help you understand your own brother.

I've seen Jack wandering around with his camera and I've waved but kept moving – usually in the opposite direction. Things with Jack have changed. It's unclassifiable. They've changed with Elsie too. She was my best friend, and now I don't know if we're friends at all. All this anguish because we both said careless things.

'I never knew Elsie was called Berry-Brown,' says Juna when I mention Elsie's name.

'Me neither,' says Cooper. 'I thought it was just Berry.'

They look at me blankly and I start to doubt myself.

'No, that's her name,' I insist. 'Berry is her mum's

surname, and Brown is her dad's – except she doesn't see her dad anymore.'

My tummy flips. One of the last things I said to Elsie was, *you don't even have a dad.* What a rotten thing to say.

'What's wrong, Ellie,' asks Juna. I glance at Cooper. He was there when I said it.

I swallow. 'I told Elsie that she didn't have a dad.'

'Everyone has a father, *somehow,*' says Juna, gently.

'I know,' I say, feeling ashamed.

It's half past six. I take the DECT phone and ring Elsie's mobile. The call goes straight to voicemail and, to be honest, I'm relieved. My mouth is dry. I hang up without leaving a message.

'What should I do?' I ask Juna.

'Follow through with a text.'

I go to find Eddie. He's slumped on the sofa in the den with his eyes shut. Susie Q*, an ancient song, blares out. This song influenced Eddie to buy the boat as a surprise for Susannah. Because he loves her. Very much. He's missing her. Obviously.

I nudge him. He snaps off the music with the remote and rearranges his face, so he looks less unhappy.

'What is it, Chicken?'

'Can I text Elsie, please?'

'Sure,' he says, giving me his smartphone.

I hover, then ask: 'Are you all right, Eddie?'

'I was your age when you were born,' he says, changing the subject. 'I thought a baby sister would be gross.'

Understandable. I felt that way about Fin. Babies stink.

'But –' Eddie gives me a true smile '– it was exactly the opposite.'

It's a compliment and I'll run with it. I am the opposite of gross.

'Thanks, Eddie,' I say. 'You're not gross either.'

Eddie splutters then says, 'That means a lot.'

I take Eddie's mobile to my bedroom and text Elsie.

Hi Elsie. U R right. I shouldn't have said what I said about your dad. I am sorry. I just want 2 B friends.

I send the text and hope that Elsie will forgive me.

No more second chances

We just want a nice, ordinary day. We've packed a picnic and it's hot outside. We meet Cooper at the end of the promenade and make our way across the cornfield towards Portis Crag. Herman smells the sea and its pull is irresistible. He trots joyfully along the track and scrambles under the stile. When we catch up, we see Herman, ears flattened, looking confused and upset. Abigail is perched on the wall, a sketch of meanness. Jack stands close by looking angry. Herman's tail, tucked between his legs, makes small, apologetic splashes.

'What happened?' I ask.

Jack strokes Herman's head and looks at Abigail coldly.

'Abigail caught him with her foot,' says Jack, carefully. 'Are you all right, boy?' he asks Herman.

'You kicked Herman?' I gasp.

'It was going to bite me,' says Abigail.

'Herman's not an *it,* and he wouldn't bite anyone,' says Cooper, crossly.

Herman looks at me, full of remorse. He's like that. When things go wrong, he only ever blames himself. I hug him and kiss his head.

'Gross,' says Abigail, wrinkling her nose in disgust.

'No. Not gross! Exactly the opposite of gross,' I say.

Juna puts her hand on my shoulder and tugs slightly.

We walk away – Herman at my heels glancing back anxiously, expecting more trouble.

'No more second chances,' I say.

Cooper and Juna nod. They know exactly what I mean. Abigail has totally blown it.

We climb aboard the Susie Q. Juna carries Tilly, but Herman has lost his bounce and hovers on the jetty.

'It's all right, Herman. I'm angry with Abigail, not you. You did nothing wrong. You're a good boy,' Cooper tells him.

Herman rallies, leaps aboard and sinks down, resting his chin on Cooper's foot.

Honestly, I could hug Cooper. The sea ripples and Susie Q rocks gently. I slide back the hatch and climb down the ladder into the cabin. There are biscuit crumbs on the galley counter. Eddie must have been back.

From the jetty I hear: 'Permission to come aboard, Cap'n?'

It's Jack. I'll have to talk to him now. I unpack our picnic. There's a bag of rice bones for Herman and Tilly. Eddie thought of everything.

I take a deep breath and climb back on deck. Juna and Jack are already deep in conversation. For a moment, a sunbeam ignites the space between them. There was a time when Juna rarely spoke, but she's different now. That makes me happy, but the way they laugh together makes me feel sort of... sad.

'Oh no,' says Cooper, under his breath.

Coming down the jetty is Bella, Abigail and a reluctant

Gilby who looks, if truth be told, a bit vulnerable.

It's only half past eight and already I'm in my PJs. I'm EXHAUSTED. What a strange day! Imagine the scene: the gentle rocking of the boat; the sound of waves lapping against the harbour wall. Soothing? Er... *No!*

Brief recap:

* Bella explained she was on her way to see me: 'I *know* where you live,' she said, making it sound like a threat. Apparently, she wanted to apologise for our 'misunderstanding', although, come to think of it, she never actually apologised. En route, she saw Abigail, who told her we'd come down to the harbour. Then, who should they bump into, but Gilby, looking like he'd 'lost his teddy,' so Bella dragged him along. Thanks Bella!

* Bella mocked Gilby, poked him in the ribs, then rubbernecked her attention on Jack who seemed, I'm irritated to say, flattered. Ugh!

* Gilby went bright red and refused to make eye contact with anyone.

* Somehow Bella managed to wedge herself between Juna and Jack and played swing-ball with her hair, all the while talking, talking, talking.

* Abigail sat opposite Jack, biting her nails and throwing shade at everyone.

* Juna spent her time trying to avoid mouthfuls of Bella's hair.

* Cooper served the food without saying a word, then spent a long time tidying the galley.

* Herman ate Bella's sandwich which she'd rejected because it wasn't the 'right cheese.' He wanted to be friends with Bella until she called him 'stupid' again. After that, he flattened his ears and turned his back on her – rightly so.

* For a while I fixated on Gilby's scarred leg and thought about all the stress he had inflicted on my life.

Throughout the afternoon Juna and I exchanged looks and silent conversation. *How is this happening?* we asked one another. *Are we really socializing with Gilby? Does Bella ever stop talking?* It was hard not to notice Bella's sun-kissed skin and perfect smile. I was conscious of my extremely efficient ears and covered them with my hair. Then Bella started making plans for all of us.

'We'll have a barbeque and we'll go in the jacuzzi,' swished Bella, oblivious to the lack of enthusiasm from everyone except Jack. And, as easy as that, I regret to inform you, we got roped in to going back to the Bitter Regret hotel *again.*

Accepting invitations graciously is a side-effect of being brought up to be polite and today, it sucked.

***

03:00 hours

Awake. Anxious. Juna asleep. Tilly asleep. Herman
snoring. Tiptoe downstairs. Under the captain's
chest in a dark, dusty space is the 'All Alone and
Abandoned' Rule Book.
Question: Will fifty rules (created by my parents –
so they'll be flawed, let's face it) help me? Will
they make things worse? Confuse me? Overwhelm me?

I climb the stairs and get back into bed. It's times like
these when it's good to have someone to reach out to. I
close my eyes and concentrate, launching my thoughts
into the balmy night – *Susannah. Where are you? I miss
our talks. Please come back...*

Eddie's personal stuff

It's early. Eddie's chopping fruit and throwing it into the blender. Juna's getting dressed, so it's just me and him.

'Eddie...'

'Hmm?'

'Does Susannah know *how* much you love her?'

I'm thinking of the time when I snooped and found the 'I ♡ U' message in the lighthouse.* I never did own up to that. My guilty conscience creeps up and bites me and I burst into tears. I get up and put my arms around him, my head against his chest.

'I miss Susannah.' Loss is painful. That's why it's called heartache.

Juna opens the kitchen door, sees us and retreats.

'Susannah can't *not* love you, Eddie. You're not bad. I mean, you're better than you used to be. And there's *no* reason why she can't still be friends with *me.*'

Eddie laughs sadly. He seems to make a decision: my brother is going to discuss personal stuff with me and I'm not sure I'm ready. I've spent years trying to avoid conversations with Eddie.

We go into the garden and sit at the table, facing one another.

'We had a fundamental disagreement,' says Eddie. 'It

was make or break –' his voice falters '– and we broke.'

'But why?' I ask, panicked. It sounds so painful and final.

'Susannah wants to travel,' says Eddie.

That's not a bad thing, I think. That's what adventurous people do.

'She wanted me to go with her–'

Oh, here comes the crunch.

'–and I said, no.'

'Why?'

Eddie looks at his hands. He has long fingers, like Grandma. How strange that such different people can be so alike. We are family, after all.

'It was too abrupt and I thought... you might need me.'

I swallow hard and look away. A couple of weeks ago, I would have packed his bags for him.

'I want to be there for you, Ellie – and Fin's so young. I want him to know I'm his brother.'

I gulp. These heart-to-hearts are a bit *much*.

'But why would Susannah have a problem with that?' I ask, nervously.

'Because,' says Eddie slowly, 'she asked me to choose.'

And there it is, in a nutshell. Eddie, who loves Susannah so much, chose me and the sticky Finster. Suddenly, family, friendship and love feel like a whole different ball game – one with complicated rules and sacrifice. I'm still processing this thought when Grandma wafts into the garden. She studies us for a moment, then squeezes Eddie's shoulder. Eddie leans into her and she wraps her arms around him. I never knew they loved one

71

another so much. *Does Grandma have two apples of her eye?*

She sits under the magnolia tree and breathes deeply. 'Life. It's complicated. Adapt and survive,' she says softly.

This must be an important rule, because it's true. I'm getting used to Grandma racing off in her biscuit tin car, and I'm fine with Juna and Eddie for company.

Juna comes out of the house with Herman and Tilly. The dogs settle together in the shade.

'I went to see Jenny Williams in the hospital. She might have a few trial days at home,' says Grandma.

Oh. That might have implications. Juna's staying to support Tilly while Mrs Williams is in hospital. At least, that's what we've told ourselves. We look at one another, alarmed.

'If Jenny comes home, I don't think she'll be ready to look after Tilly just yet,' says Grandma. 'If you and Juna can cope a while longer, I'm sure that will be better for all concerned.'

'Oh, OK,' I say, relieved.

'Good,' says Grandma. 'Well, tally-ho.' She gets up and heads inside, probably to get ready for another day's jaunt with *Alfred.*

Adapt and survive. I guess I'm just going to have to stick that bobble on my hat and wear it.

We meet Cooper outside the Box Brownie café. We're almost on the beach when Cadence calls us back.

'I'm worried Elsie might be homesick. She sounds a bit flat. Has she said anything to you, Ellie?' asks Cadence.

I shake my head and try to avoid eye contact. I really liked Cadence. I still do, but now I feel uncomfortable with her. I have no idea if she knows Elsie and I have fallen out.

She eyes me, suspiciously. 'You *have* spoken to her?'

'Not yet,' I say in a horrible, small voice.

'Ellie's texted *and* emailed,' says Juna, defending me. 'Elsie's not replied yet, that's all.'

'She's probably busy,' I say, meekly.

Cooper stands quietly with his hands in his pockets. 'What's Elsie's surname? Is it Berry, or Berry-Brown?' he asks Cadence.

Cadence has nothing to offer other than a stony stare. It's unsettling. After an age she says, 'It's Berry. Just Berry.'

'Berry or Just *hyphen* Berry,' says Cooper, trying to joke his way out of the awkwardness.

'No *Just* and no *hyphen*,' says Cadence, curtly. 'Where on earth did you get that idea?'

Cooper and Juna look at me. I swallow, feeling like I've done something wrong. 'I must have got it wrong.'

'You did!' says Cadence then, remembering who I am – her daughter's supposed-to-be best friend – she forces a cold smile and walks away.

We hover for a moment, then run onto the beach and head for the rocks below the lighthouse. The thing Eddie found in the sand is still in my pocket. I hold it out in the palm of my hand.

'What's this fascination with you and keys?' asks Cooper.*

'Eddie found it. He gave it to me, honest.'

'I know where that's from!' cries Juna. 'It's a Little

Egret key.'

I catch my breath. The design – I see it now – a little egret's head in profile.

'Someone's lost it,' says Cooper. 'Come on. We'll go and hand it back.'

I groan. I don't want to go to the hotel again – but Cooper's right. It's lost property and we should return it.

Bella's smile dazzles. You can't help but feel a bit starstruck in her presence.

'Where's Jack?' she asks, looking past us.

Her smile evaporates when she realises he's not with us. I'm anxious and Cooper knows it. I really don't want to bump into Bella's dad – much less explain anything to him. I nudge Cooper, and slip the key into his hand.

'This was found,' he says vaguely, offering it to Bella, who glances but can't be bothered to look. We follow her, like sheep, through to reception. Two Persian cats languish on the desk. I've already been put in my place by one of them.

'Hi Portia,' I say, politely, but she's not interested in me. She sticks her leg in the air as if she's playing the cello and starts to groom. I like cats – but maybe not this one so much.

'Porsche? What's your other cat called? Ferrari?' jokes Cooper. Eden, tucked in a corner with a Nintendo, sniggers.

'Portia, the Shakespearian heroine, *not* Porsche the dumb car,' snaps Bella contemptuously.

'The Merchant of Venice,' says Cooper. 'All that glisters

is not gold.'*

Bella is rattled that Cooper can quote Shakespeare.

'The other one is Juliette... *another* Shakespeare character,' chimes Eden, without looking up.

'Is there a Romeo?' asks Cooper.

'Bella pushed him off a balcony. S-p-*lat*.'

'There is no Romeo,' states Bella – then to Eden, 'Clear off or I'll splat you!'

Oh boy! Am I completely through with verbally abusing my brothers. It's ugly.

Bella goes behind the reception desk and pulls out a heavy box full of egret keys.

'We've had keypads installed. We are now a *keyless* environment.'

'What a shame,' says Juna. 'They're beautiful.'

'Keys are old fashioned,' says Bella, 'and anyway, morons lose them, or *steal* them. Throw it in there,' she says, irritated, 'or keep it. I don't care.'

'Really? Thanks,' says Cooper, pleased.

Bella looks at Cooper critically. His appearance, always clean, sometimes signals the lack of money in his family.

'Help yourself. They're not worth anything in case you were wondering,' she says.

Cooper flushes. 'They're interesting though,' he says, defiantly picking out a few more. 'Thanks again.'

I just want to escape, but it's not over. She makes us endure a miserable hour of her company. Sitting in the sun lounge sipping iced cola in tall glasses might sound relaxing, but when you all fall silent because one of you (Bella) is belligerent and patronizing – well, it's stressful and very boring.

'*Why* does Gilby like you?' she asks me suddenly.

'I'm not sure *like* is the right word,' I say, trying to be helpful. I sip my drink and end up choking – not enough to need a Heimlich manoeuvre, but pretty close.

Cooper hauls me to my feet, thwacks me on the back, sending me halfway across the room, upended on a chaise lounge. Grandma's advice was right: always wear clean underwear.

'Sorry, Ellie,' he says, shocked at his own strength. 'Are you breathing now?'

I splutter and test my lungs. 'Um, yes. Thanks, Cooper.' I right myself with not much dignity.

Eden creeps noiselessly behind Bella's chair and does bunny ears –

'Well?' snaps Bella.

– then he pulls grotesque faces, miming his sister putting on lipstick, like a pantomime dame. I struggle to suppress a giggle.

'Tell me!' she demands.

'Um, what was the question again?'

Bella eyeballs me. I try not to blink, but when I do, she's up in my face and I think she's going to slap me. Then she flounces out of the room like she's been practising that move for months.

'She does that *a lot*,' says Eden, dryly. 'Amateur dramatics.'

'And that's our cue,' says Cooper softly, 'to leave this stage and never return. To misquote Shakespeare: *Parting is not such sweet sorrow.*'

'Take me with you,' says Eden with comic timing.

'You can come with us if you want, dude,' says Cooper, kindly.

Eden shrugs. 'Someone's got to stay and supervise Queen B.'

We tumble outside into the sunshine. The day is normal and peaceful again. I glance back. What will Eden's day be like – arguing with his sister and wandering around all by himself?

'That was *c-razy,*' says Juna. 'I thought she was going to bop you.' We look at one another and pull faces, then laugh a little with relief.

'There's food on the boat,' says Cooper, because food always gives his day calm and purpose.

We make our way back to Portis Crag and head down to the harbour.

'So that's why she wanted to pick your brains, Ellie,' says Juna. 'She thinks Gilby *likes* you. How weird is that? What has he *said* to her?'

'Whatever it is, that girl's got "*issues,*"' says Cooper, using his fingers as quotation marks.

'She's jealous,' says Juna.

'Bella's not jealous of me!' I can't believe it. *Would anyone want my ears?* 'Do you think Eden's OK?' I ask. I recognised his smile. It didn't come from a happy place.

We walk through the harbour car park and see Jack on the jetty.

'Oh no!' I groan.

Cooper looks at me strangely.

I sigh. 'I've had enough of people today.'

'Thanks!' says Cooper.

'Not you, dope.'

'Thanks again,' he says.

Jack waves and walks over to join us. We climb aboard Susie Q and Cooper goes below deck to organise snacks. Jack falls into conversation with Juna. They talk about light and composition. They're both artistic so it makes sense they share interests. Then Jack turns to me and smiles, and my spirits lift a little.

'Gilby's dad is a git!' he says, cheerfully.

'State the obvious, why don't you,' says Cooper, emerging with a tray.

'He practically ran me down – jumped out of his car, told me the hotel mustn't have any negative publicity, and ordered me to delete any photos I'd taken of the hotel from my camera.'

'And did you?' I ask, shocked.

'No, I challenged him to a fist fight,' says Jack, ripping open a bag of Hula Hoops and stuffing a handful in his mouth.

I'm not used to flippant Jack. The reason why grown-ups like him so much is because he's the exact opposite of flippant.

'Sorry, Ellie,' he says, responding to my expression. 'Yeah, I deleted them. I felt a bit... threatened.'

'And there's a new psycho on the block. Bella got in Ellie's face just now.'

'*Bellissima* Bella?' asks Jack, incredulous.

I'm slightly crestfallen.

'No. Belligerent, bombastic, *bop-your-face* Bella,' says

Cooper, annoyed.

Juna tells Jack what happened. Her voice is calming, and the cross-dynamics settle down. Susie Q dips and bobs as the tide comes in. The conversation circles back to the attack on the Little Egret hotel.

'Bitter regret? What does it mean, anyway?' asks Juna. 'Who regrets what?'

'Well, it's nothing to do with Bella's theory that the hotel is haunted,' I say. 'Ghosts don't drag ladders and slosh paint.'

'Bella's dad might have enemies. He's not exactly *Signore* Nice Guy,' says Jack.

'Enemies? That's scary,' I say – thinking of the people who fall into that category for me. Gilby, for sure. Abigail – she kicked my dog. Bella got in my face. Alfred – he's stealing my grandma.

'Bella thinks Gilby *likes* me. She put the saddle on the wrong end of *that* donkey.'

'What is the wrong end of a donkey?' asks Cooper.

'The opposite of the right end.'

'It's crazy season,' says Jack.

'Maybe,' I say wondering what's going to happen next. Life's not predictable since my parents flew away and the wind of change began to blow.

The breeze picks up and we make a move.

'Always leave a place better than you found it,' says Cooper, wiping the top of the galley counter. 'Eddie's got a secret biscuit habit,' he says. 'Crumbs everywhere.'

'It's a shame about the Bitter Regret photographs,' I say to Jack. 'You shouldn't really destroy evidence.'

'Good job they're backed up then,' says Jack.

'You've got copies?'

'D-uh. I'm not playing by his rules and he's not ordering me around. I make my own decisions,' says Jack, sounding pretty grown-up.

I think of the *'All Alone and Abandoned' Rule Book*, collecting dust under the captain's chest. I feel a pang of shame that I've not read it, but at least now I know why. I am like Jack. I want to make my own decisions.

The first storm

I wake up to a lightning flash. I count four seconds before the thunder crashes. God is moving his furniture around. That's what Grandma told me when I was small, and I believed it for a while. Juna sleeps on, but Tilly is agitated. Storms have been forecast this week: hot and calm through the day – thunder, lightning and rough seas at night.

It's after midnight. I get out of bed to watch for the next fork of lightning. Cadence has left out a parasol. It looks spooky wedged against the side of the café, flapping wildly in the wind. I could wake Eddie and ask him to rescue it, before it blows away – but Elsie won't communicate with me, so I'm not sure I should bother. I'm hurt, I'm young, and yes, I'm immature sometimes.

I shouldn't have said that she didn't have a dad, but how many times can I say sorry? And now Cadence is upset with me. Did I dream that Elsie's name was Berry-Brown? Wait... I search my desk. There it is – my notebook with the glittery cover. I flick through the pages. In indigo ink: *Elsie Mabel Berry-Brown** is written in Elsie's handwriting. Underneath it: *Menella Edith Booton*, in mine. When Elsie and I first met, this was how we introduced ourselves.

'*Berry is my mum's name and Brown is my dad's, though I don't see my dad anymore.*' She said this. It is not fake news. But why did Elsie lie about her name?

I'm restless. I go downstairs to the kitchen for a glass of water. Tilly follows on my heels and jumps up on Grandma's chair which is cosy with cushions and a crocheted blanket. I'm surprised when Grandma, yawning, walks in.

'Cracking storm,' says Grandma. 'Did it wake you too?'

I don't feel chatty. I'm tired and it's strange feeling uncertain about Grandma. If ever I needed a sane, reliable adult in my life, she was always my best bet – but that was before Alfred stole her away. There's another flash of lightning. The air between us is static.

'How are you doing, Ellie?' asks Grandma gently.

'Do you *really* want to know?' I ask. The quiet hostility in my voice shocks me.

Grandma hears it too, but she's good at not reacting. She pats Tilly on the head and chooses another chair. She waits...

Thunder rumbles across the sky and into the house. I can feel it in my chest. Tilly looks at us and flattens her ears. I'm not sure if she's disturbed by the storm, or me. I think of Elsie marching away along the cliff top; how shocked I was when we came across the Bitter Regret sign; how weird I felt when I saw the photo of Jack and Alex; how my stomach flipped when, through the corn stalks, I heard Gilby sobbing; and the rush of adrenaline when Bella got in my face. So many things happen now that I don't share with Grandma. Juna said Bella was jealous. That doesn't seem likely though I think I might be jealous of Alfred, whoever he is. Grandma is mine, not his. Jealousy is a new emotion for me and it's not an easy one to experience. Grandma watches me, searching my face.

'I am impressed with you, Ellie,' she says.

'You *are?*'

'You're coping so well.'

'I *am?*'

That's not what I expected. I'm hovering on failure. My good nature is brittle, about to snap, and I seem to have lost direction.

'Your parents and Fin disappear into the ether but, still, you crack on with life,' says Grandma, seriously. 'You're doing jobs around the house and getting along with Eddie. You're helping to look after Tilly, you're a great support to Cooper, and you're creating a real friendship with Juna.' Grandma spreads her hands wide. 'Whatever challenge you face, you do your best. What more could anyone ask?'

I absorb this news about myself. It doesn't feel accurate but then Grandma has always been good at putting a positive spin on things.

'I'm getting it wrong sometimes, Grandma,' I say.

'Well, who's perfect?' she says in the voice of reason I have relied on for so long.

'Thanks Grandma,' I say, with a lump in my throat.

The air between us settles a little.

'You can ask how I'm doing, if you like,' says Grandma.

I think. I don't want to ask anything about Alfred. Instead, I ask Grandma if she is lonely.

Grandma is surprised. She takes a deep breath and her

hand flutters across her heart.

'I'm doing better, Ellie,' she says. 'It's hard living my life without your Grandpa. I miss my best friend.'

The sadness in her voice crushes me. I always thought Grandma's job was to be there for me. I never really thought about someone being there for her.

'I'll be your best friend, Grandma,' I say. My throat stings. I miss Grandpa too.

'It's more than enough that you're my granddaughter,' says Grandma. 'All you have to be is your own sound self.'

'Am I sound?' I ask.

'Of course. You always work things out.'

For a nanosecond, I glimpse my future and know that, no matter what happens, I will always try to work things out.

Grandma is right – and it's good to know that she thinks I'm sound – even if sometimes I struggle. I *can* put my best foot forward. I *am* growing up.

Grandma rummages in the fridge, eats a piece of cheese and wanders back to bed. Eddie's laptop is on the kitchen table. I'm not going to give up on Elsie – she was my first friend in this town.

Email:

Hi Elsie
I am truly sorry. I hope one day you'll trust me with the story of your dad.
Miss you lots.
Love, Ellie x

I find Eddie asleep on the sofa in the den, still plugged into music. I pull out his earphones. A song called *Paint It Black** is playing. I wish he wouldn't listen to such bleak lyrics.

'Eddie... *Eddie!*'

He shakes himself awake. 'What's wrong?' he asks, alarmed.

'I need you to do something.'

'What?'

'Cadence left a parasol out and there's a storm.'

'You want me to get it?'

'Please.'

'All right,' says Eddie, already standing up.

Now let's be real. How many adults (because Eddie is, technically, an adult) would brave a storm in the middle of the night to chase a parasol? Not many.

There's another lightning flash and two seconds later a clap of thunder shakes the house. Tilly is agitated and paws at the door.

'Storm's moving closer. Look after Tilly. I'll be back in a mo, if I don't get struck by lightning.' He sees the look on my face. 'Joking. There's only a fifty per cent chance I'll get frazzled to a crisp.'

'Really?' I ask, worried.

Eddie laughs, pulls on his jacket and steps into the storm. Anxious, I watch from the window. Ten minutes later, I strain to see him tango up the hill with the parasol fighting him every step of the way. He tumbles inside, drenched.

'Well, that was a barrel of laughs,' he says, shaking off

the raindrops. Then I notice he's actually shaking.

'What is it?' I ask.

He props the parasol against Dad's office door to drip-dry.

'Nothing.'

That didn't sound convincing.

'I thought I saw something.'

'Saw what?'

'Nothing. Go to bed, Ellie. It's late.'

No one could ever call Eddie a chatterbox. He's done talking for the night. At least the parasol signifies progress. Tomorrow, Juna and I can carry it down to the Box Brownie café and Cadence will be grateful. It will start the process of putting things right.

When regret is bitter

I wake up to a slobbery kiss. I love Herman, but not his dog breath. Juna prods my shoulder.

'You'll never guess who's downstairs?'

'Darth Vader?' I say, yawning.

'Good guess. Eden,' says Juna, pulling a face.

'What's he doing here?'

'He's come to see you. Eddie gave him breakfast. He had the cheek to rate it one-star. Get dressed! I don't know how to talk to him.'

'How hard can it be?' I ask. I know everything there is to know about younger brothers. Conversation isn't a priority. They're usually too busy trying to dislodge the Lego they've stuffed up their noses or else trying to impress someone with a burp.

I haven't had enough sleep and I'm grumpy. I pull on shorts and a T-shirt then head downstairs, barefoot.

'Wow,' says Eden, eyeing me. 'You go to a *lot* of trouble.'

'Pardon?'

'Ever heard of a hairbrush?'

'That's not polite, dude,' says Eddie, who hasn't combed his hair in a week.

'Sorry,' says Eden, sounding not sorry. 'Don't you ever

87

put goo on your face?'

'Goo?' I gulp. I am under attack.

Eden pulls a comedy face and puts on imaginary lipstick. It's funny and mortifying at the same time. I flush, horribly aware of myself.

'Goo's revolting. Anyway, it wouldn't work on you,' he says matter-of-factly. He turns to Eddie. 'I'm giving her a sort of compliment.'

'OK,' says Eddie, doubtfully.

Juna gives me a knowing look. 'Nightmare,' she mouths.

'Here's your one-star breakfast,' says Eddie giving Eden the side-eye. He plonks a bowl of Rice Krispies topped with raspberries in front of me. 'Get your gnashers around that.'

Eden watches me, fascinated. I sit down and start to chomp defiantly. I am saved by the doorbell.

Cooper shouts, 'Only me,' and strolls into the kitchen. He sees Eden and does a double take.

'Do you always hang out with *girls?*' asks Eden, rudely.

'I understand why you're jealous,' quips Cooper, then to me, 'I guess you've heard?'

'Heard what?'

'The Egret's been attacked again.'

We all gasp – except Eden.

'Oh yeah,' he says, smirking. '*That's* what I came here to tell you.'

'Have you seen it?' I ask Cooper.

He shakes his head and hands me his phone. It's a message from Jack.

Taking sunrise pix this morning. Saw this –

There's a photo of the Little Egret Hotel. It's been graffitied with Bitter Regret *again*. I pass the phone to Juna and Eddie.

'Someone is out to get the Vittori family,' says Eddie.

There's an awkward silence. This affects Eden.

'Are you OK?' I ask him.

'Sure,' he says. 'It's just an average day in Crazy Town.'

Eden leans in to look at the photo. 'Funny how Jack just happened to be there,' he says, frowning. 'And he shouldn't have taken photos. Dad will go–' Eden mimes a crazed ape.

Eddie sighs and eyeballs me. 'You might not want to hear this now,' he says. 'Grandma wondered whether we'd like to join her for coffee and cake at the Little Egret this morning.'

'*Coffee?*' I say, disgusted. I don't drink coffee – but seriously, was this *really* my first thought?

'Milkshake? Fruit juice?' says Eddie, annoyed. 'What you drink isn't important.'

I know that. More horrible than coffee and the Bitter Regret attack on the hotel, is the thought of meeting Alfred.

Of course, everyone is included. We pile into Eddie's Skoda which Eden rates as *minus one-star and pathetic.* I'm just grateful the brakes work and it hardly stinks.

'Nothing wrong with being opinionated,' says Eddie to Eden. 'Just try not to insult people more than three times in one sitting.'

Eddie's car crawls up the steep hotel drive. We park next to a white van loaded with ladders. Two workers in overalls prepare to paint over the graffiti and blot out the Bitter Regret attack.

Outside the entrance, Mr. Vittori stands stiffly on guard.

'No photographs, please,' he says coldly. He looks through us, which allows Eden to skirt around his own father, unnoticed.

'Do you want to join us, Eden?' asks Eddie.

'You'll like Ellie's grandma,' says Juna. 'She's a sculptor.'

I feel a glow of pride, ruined by Eden's mocking tone: 'A *sculpture?*' Another mime – it's not flattering, and Grandma would never pull a shape like that.

'That's enough, dude. Don't disrespect our grandmother,' says Eddie with a touch of steel in his voice.

Eden hesitates. 'Sorry. I'll show you where to go.'

We follow Eden obediently, skirting alongside the pool, through a rose garden before Cooper says, 'We're going in a circle.'

Eden legs it, howling. We hear him shout, 'Suckers!'

'What a twonk,' says Cooper under his breath.

I laugh then wonder, why *does* Cooper spend so much time with us? I don't have to say it out loud.

Cooper shrugs. 'Because we're friends, Ellie,' he says.

Notes on 'coffee and cake'

* Alfred is too old to be called a 'boyfriend.'
* Alfred is too smiley and polite, and far too interested in my grandma, for me to like him.
* Alfred and Eddie were far too chatty. I decided their conversation didn't interest me and studied the menu instead.
* Alfred suggested Juna and I should try a melon and raspberry milkshake, so I asserted myself and ordered an energy drink with dental damaging properties. (It made me feel weird and gave me wind.)
* I refused to make eye contact with Alfred and Grandma – and I knew, without anyone telling me, that **I had not done my best on this occasion.**

Juna and I carry the parasol down the hill to the Box Brownie café. Cadence sees us, approaches, but I hesitate a moment too long, so Juna steps in and tells her that Eddie rescued it from the storm.

'How thoughtful. He's so kind. Tell Eddie, thank you,' says Cadence and twirls off with a tray of cheese toasties.

I don't need thanking, obviously. I'm just the fool who spotted the *stupid parasol* in the first place.

'What's wrong, Ellie?' asks Juna looking worried.

We're back in the garden sitting on the rickety bench.

'Nothing.' I'm tired, upset and confused – not a good combination of feelings. It's overwhelming and, in my mind, I start to walk away from myself.

Herman slumps in the shade of the magnolia tree with his back to me. I hear Juna sigh. We sit, not speaking. Bees drone in the lavender. The peace of the day irritates me, and I am perfectly miserable.

'Have I done something wrong?' asks Juna at last.

Here's my opportunity to turn this dark mood around – but I'm too stubborn to take it.

'No,' I say coldly.

Time goes by. I keep my eyes fixed on a cargo boat on the horizon, trying to work out how many metres it moves every minute. It's impossible to assess, but it diverts my attention from my bad-tempered self.

I will speak to Juna when the boat is in line with the edge of the rocks by the lighthouse. It takes an age for it to get there. I force myself to wait, and when I turn to Juna, there's empty space. Even Herman has left me.

I creep into the house. Eddie's in the workshop but there's no sign of Juna. I open my bedroom door, afraid she will not be there. The first thing I see is her bag, neatly packed with all her stuff. Juna looks up from her book. She smiles sadly and stands up.

'I'll go home now, Ellie. Thanks for letting me stay with you,' she says awkwardly. 'Tilly will be OK now she knows you. She'll be able to go home soon anyway.'

Juna bends down and kisses Tilly's head. 'Be good,' she says, then to me, 'Can I give you a hug?'

I cannot speak. I don't want Juna to go. I don't want to be mean. *I don't want any of this.*

Juna hesitates, but I can't look at her. She picks up her bag and heads to the door.

I cannot move. *No, Juna! I'm sorry. Read my thoughts, please.*

Gently, she closes the door behind her. The stairs creak. The front door opens and closes. She walks down the garden path and through the gate. Her bag is heavy and it's a long walk home. How must she feel?

I've ruined everything. I climb on my bed and begin to count the petals on the wallpaper. If I can count a thousand, I may feel calmer.

I don't know what time it is. There's a gentle knock on my door.

781, 782, 783, 784 –

Eddie comes in. From his look, I know it is time to stop counting.

'I'm not sound,' I say, surprised I can still speak. *Why would I hurt Juna, when life has already hurt her plenty?*

I climb on the window seat and look directly into Eddie's eyes. *Please find me, Eddie. I am lost. Grandma told me I was sound – but I'm not and I'm frightened.*

'Juna's gone,' I tell him.

'She's downstairs,' says Eddie. 'I saw her go and went after her. She knows you're having a rough day. She just wants to be friends.'

His stillness draws me in. I melt against him and cry into his hair.

'Chicken,' says Eddie softly.

He's not angry. *He should be angry, I'm sure he should.*

'You are imperfectly sound. It will be OK,' he says, hugging me tightly.

'Was I horrible to Alfred as well?' I ask.

'Pretty much,' says Eddie.

I always had the idea that I was polite and kind – but I'm not. I can be horrible.

'We'll work it out. Come downstairs.'

'What do I say to her?'

'What do you think you should say?'

'Sorry.'

'Exactly.'

Eddie and gravity pull me downstairs. I say sorry to Juna, who is not stubborn. She hugs me. I cry. She hugs me some more. We go into the garden and eat strawberries and ice cream. Eddie and Juna are normal and kind, so I pull my face into a better shape and I begin to find my way back into my own skin.

Later on, Cooper comes over. He eats with us, always grateful for food and company. He chats with Juna and Eddie about Alfred who had an interesting job, apparently. I missed the detail because I was too busy being hostile and rude.

The shame of the day presses me. I *regret* it. *Bitterly.* Eye contact feels unnatural. Juna follows Tilly inside and Eddie goes to tidy the workshop. Cooper and I are left to watch the sun sink into the sea.

'You OK?' asks Cooper eventually.

I nod, not looking at him. I'm not sure I'm OK.

'Are *we* OK?' he asks.

The anxiety in his voice shocks me. Cooper's life is not straightforward. His friends are important to him, which means I am important too.

'I'm sorry,' I say.

'What for?' he asks.

'For being ratty with everyone.'

'I hadn't noticed,' he says in his deadpan voice, then smiles in a way that makes him family to me.

Something unearthly

This is the day after yesterday, which wasn't good. I'm hoping for a stabilizing, peaceful day.

Grandma is in the garden and I hurry downstairs to join her before she disappears. I am braced to offer a grovelling apology for being an obnoxious kid. Good, sound people take responsibility for their actions and I will take responsibility for mine.

Grandma munches her toast like a finalist in the breakfast Olympics. She's in a hurry – maybe to go and see Alfred – maybe to get away from me. I sit next to her, anxiously.

'Good morning, Grandma,' I say politely.

Grandma holds the local paper, the Peregrine Post, which we use to line the swing bin in the kitchen.

'Take a look at this!' demands Grandma, licking her fingers and slapping the page.

I gasp. Making a splash on the front page under the headline: **MYSTERIOUS ATTACKS ON LOCAL HOTEL**, is a photo of the BITTER REGRET attack. We look at one another open mouthed.

'What's going on? I thought they wanted to keep it quiet.'

'I've got the wrong specs on. Read it out loud,'

commands Grandma.

'During the night, the Little Egret Hotel was targeted by an act of vandalism. The hotel sign was defaced with red paint and altered to read, Bitter Regret. This is the second such attack in one week. Co-owner, Vincent Vittori commented, "I have no idea why anyone would do this. We are the proud new owners of this hotel and I know there is certainly no reason, now nor in the past, for patrons to ever regret, much less bitterly regret, their stay here. The standard of our accommodation and service is second to none and as far as we are concerned, it is business as usual." [Continued on page 4]'

I turn to page 4. Grandma balances her glasses on the tip of her nose and squints.

'You'd need nerves of steel to dangle from a ladder and slosh paint around in the middle of the night. Go on, read the rest,' commands Grandma.

'PR Consultant, Liam Flynn, a local man advising the hotel's owners—'

'Is he anything to do with Gilby Flynn?' asks Grandma.

'His dad.'

'Good grief!'

'Um ... Liam Flynn, a local man, blah, blah, blah, has recommended upgrades to the hotel's security, including the installation of closed-circuit television, which is currently being undertaken. Said Mr. Flynn, "It is unfortunate that CCTV was not operational at the time of the attacks –"'

'That's a shame,' says Grandma.

'"My client is badly shaken, and we feel these wanton acts of vandalism may have been motivated by jealousy, as the Little Egret has an enviable reputation along this coastline."'

'Seriously? That's insulting to other hotel owners. He's almost accusing them. That's not good PR,' says Grandma.

'Said Mr. Vittori, "We will not be intimidated. This unpleasant experience has prompted me to commence a program of refurbishment. I envision a streamlined, updated, and even more luxurious feel to the hotel, whilst still making the most of its beautiful Georgian features."'

'Good on him... I guess,' says Grandma doubtfully.

'The Little Egret Hotel was built in 1790 for Stephen and Catherine Luxton, and was originally known as Luxton Hall. Its location, on the hill above the local beauty spot known as Portis Crag –'

'Get to the juicy bits, Ellie,' interrupts Grandma, slurping tea.

'Um... Blah, blah, blah... It may come as a shock to local people that there are plans to change the hotel's name to symbolise a fresh start. Said Mr. Vittori, "Due to this unwelcome and negative publicity, we feel it is necessary to change the hotel's name which will involve, unfortunately, removing the sign on the front of the building and the little egret weathervane. Locals and patrons need not worry. The Little Egret's demise means the birth of something even better."'

'That's insane!' says Grandma, irritated. 'It's not the Little Egret's fault.'

The garden gate creaks and Cooper swings through.

'Mornin',' he calls.

Grandma pats the chair beside her and Cooper heads over.

'I like your outfit,' says Cooper.

Grandma, in cropped linen trousers and a loose cotton

top printed with peacocks, looks summery and fresh.

'Charmer,' says Grandma, who gets over irritations very quickly. 'There's plenty of tea in the pot. Tuck in. Damson or strawberry?'

'Thanks, Mrs. B. I'll give damson a shot,' says Cooper, already buttering toast. Grandma plonks the jam in front of him and Cooper flashes her an easy smile. He's come a long way since he first met her. If I remember correctly, she fed him then, too. Lemon drizzle cake. He's loved her ever since.

Grandma stands and rests her hand on my shoulder.

'How lucky to be young, carefree, and have such good friends. You are truly blessed, Ellie Booton.'

I tilt my head and touch her hand with my cheek, grateful for this normal, loving moment. I can be an obnoxious kid, but Grandma loves me. I am not always carefree, but I am young and I have good friends. For now, my world feels steady again.

'Have a good time on the boat. Mobile's on if you need me,' calls Grandma, disappearing into the house.

Today, I am almost glad she has Alfred to keep her company and I am grateful Cooper's here. I fold the paper back to the front page and push it in front of him.

He stops mid-bite. 'I thought they wanted to keep it quiet?'

'Exactly. That's what I said.'

We're aboard the Susie Q, a mile from shore. Eddie's done a Coastal Skipper course and now my brother who, for years, wouldn't get close enough to water to wash, hated school and almost bummed out of college, is teaching Cooper and me how to sail – and he's good at it. He's even organised life jackets for Herman and Tilly! Jack, of course, is taking photographs. Juna is sketching. The sea is smooth and there's a fresh south-westerly that blasts our headspace with clean, cool air and good thoughts. I'm learning the ropes and we're bombing along. From the boat, the Little Egret's weathervane is visible above Portis Crag. I wonder what Bella is doing. Sunbathing by the pool? Having her nails done? Whatever it is, she will look amazing – but this is not a day to worry about my appearance. I'm windblown and happy and my friends are worth their weight in gold. The wind of change. I'm going with the flow and I am growing up. I laugh out loud and high five Cooper. Herman wags his tail and snorts the salty air. He is a sea dog at heart.

I'm writing this in bed. It's been an exhausting day and I've worked hard. The boat bumped and rocked across the sea, but my world felt steady and safe again – until Cooper ran back to the house looking like he'd seen a ghost, which maybe he had. Peace never lasts long. This is what happened...

Eddie made us vegan pizza. It couldn't have been nicer. We sat in the garden chomping away, joking around. Jack and I took monkey face selfies together on his phone and I didn't once think about Alex (the girl in the photo with Jack). Jack wanted to get a sunset shot of the Little Egret's weathervane, so he left first. By the time Cooper left, there was a full moon to light his way. Juna and I were in our

PJs when we heard something slam against the front door.

We charged downstairs – Eddie got there first – and Cooper fell into the house as white as a sheet. This is what he told us: It started to rain. The wind had picked up and a patchy sea fret rolled in reducing visibility, so he ran for home, taking the shortcut across the cornfield. He managed to locate the stile and climb over just as someone, or *something*, cried out. For a moment, the moon reappeared and in front of him was a figure 'hovering' in the mist. He vaulted back over the stile and ran for his life.

Cooper kept apologising. I noticed he'd torn his jeans, somehow. We reassured him that he was completely right to run back ~~ho~~ here. I nearly wrote *home*. This is Cooper's second home. Anyway, in my family, tea and toast is the standard treatment for stress or shock, so Eddie made toast, a pot of tea (Cherry Good for me) and Herman sat quietly with his chin on Cooper's knee to comfort him.

Eddie offered to walk to Portis Crag to take a look. No one was in favour of that, especially Cooper, and frankly, Eddie seemed relieved. I asked Eddie what he'd seen the other night. '*When?*' he asked, though Eddie knew exactly when – the night he tangoed with the parasol. Then he told us he wasn't sure *what* he'd seen. Something *alive*. Something *flowing*. Cooper thought *flowing* was the right word. It was *unearthly, he* said. Then we discussed whether we should call the police, but no one was in favour of that either. PC Jennings has a talent for making a bad situation worse – not a good trait for a cop, really.

I told the story of how PC Jennings overreacted one

night when he nosily came across Eddie smashing stuff up with a crowbar, and how Grandma raced to the scene in her fluffy dressing gown and had to calm him down.* That made us laugh and the colour slowly crept back into Cooper's face.

'It must be awkward for Abigail having a dad like that,' Juna said.

I noticed Cooper swallow. Cooper's dad would fall asleep in front of the telly clutching a can of beer. That was a good day in their house. Other days he would shout a lot. There are many different types of awkward. My friends know stuff about families that I don't. It's always better to be around people who aren't nightmares – who will make tea and toast – who will listen, stay calm and comfort. These are the people we run to.

We started to yawn. Eddie got his car keys. In future, said Eddie, if it was dark or bad weather, he'd always give Cooper a lift home.

'I wonder what Cooper saw,' says Juna, reaching to turn the light off when we are finally ready to sleep. 'Do you believe in ghosts, Ellie?'

I don't know, but life is strange again. Cooper didn't say the word 'ghost' but the word 'unearthly' doesn't add up to something quite normal.

Life lessons and the Little Egret Friendship Society

I'm in the den reading an email from Dad.

Dear Ellie,

I phoned Grandma last night (afternoon for us) and she told me that you and Eddie are getting along famously. I immediately ordered some flags from eBay and intend to hang them out. I may organise a parade.

[Sarcasm. Big sigh.]

Grandma also said that Eddie is cooking and cleaning. It took me twenty years to convince him to shower, and longer to pick up a tea towel, and now I hear he's turned into a domestic god overnight. Maybe I should have abandoned him sooner? Tell him I will increase his pocket money when I get home. Oh, wait. He's too old to get pocket money. Too bad!

[Dad-humour can be a bit *much*.]

I assume you're desperate to know if I'm a big hit in America?

[Um, no.]

Simple answer - oh yeah! Apparently, I'm sick! (What a repulsive, absurd expression that is. I hope you never use it - except, of course, if you are about to vomit.)

[Only Dad could introduce vomit as a subject in an email.]

I'm doing radio and TV talk shows, and signings at bookshops, some the size of an English county. I'm asked about castles and cricket and they think I'm related to the Queen. Most Americans couldn't find England on the map - seriously - but that doesn't stop them from lapping it up.

[Related to the Queen? I don't *think* so. Americans can't find England on a map? Don't they go to school?]

The main point is, I'm selling books which has cheered your mum up no end. She's decided she likes shoes as much as handbags. Expensive ones.

[It's her money and he owes her a year's wages, at least.]

No need to ask if you are being good, because you usually are - so carry on kiddo and we'll see you soon.
Your loving Dad xxx
 P.S. Mum sends her love and so does Fin who, *I'm sure,* you are missing *very much.* ☺

I've adjusted to thinking of myself as *imperfectly sound,* so being labelled *usually good,* feels a bit unrealistic. I thumb through the dictionary. The definition of *good* is extremely vague.

104

good

A person or thing having the right or desired qualities; being **adequate**, satisfactory or efficient. Someone who is competent, moral, virtuous, charitable. A thing or situation that is enjoyable, **valid** or **sound.**

I can get away with being adequate, and valid – I exist, don't I? I aim to be sound. I creep into the hall feeling guilty. There are fresh flowers on the captain's chest. The *'All Alone and Abandoned' Rule Book,* is not quite where I left it. There are no dust bunnies. Someone has cleaned up and must know my secret.

I reach for the envelope, stuffed with far too many rules. How could my parents *do* this to me? Do they *want* to ruin my life?

I run upstairs and toss it onto my bunk. It slides on the duvet and gets stuck between the mattress and the wall. Great! It can be *all alone and abandoned* there instead.

Juna appears. She quietly and deliberately closes the door behind her.

'Elsie's mum is here,' she whispers. 'She wants a word.'

'With me? Am I in trouble?' The guilt of what I said to Elsie presses me.

'You've been summoned.'

We trudge downstairs. Cadence and Grandma sit at the kitchen table, not talking or drinking coffee. They're waiting... for me.

'Sit down, Ellie,' says Grandma in a serious tone.

Herman, my faithful ally, leans against me and I hold

his velvety ears for comfort. Cadence clears her throat and I am forced to look at her.

'Eddie told me it was you who asked him to rescue the parasol. I'm glad you spotted it, Ellie. They're expensive to replace. Thank you.'

That, as they say, was the good news—

'About Elsie...' begins Cadence.

—and now for the bad.

'I need to make an apology.'
That's not what I expected!
'Elsie admitted to me that she'd told you her name was Berry-Brown.'

I nod uncertainly, mesmerized. This is how Elsie will look when she's forty-something. She will be poised and beautiful. I wonder if Elsie and I will be friends when we're forty. I wonder if we'll still be friends at the end of this conversation.

'I'm sure she had her own reasons for telling you that story... but it's not true. You took the blame by saying you'd made a mistake. You were protecting her. I'm sorry I snapped at you.'

I take a deep breath. 'I said something horrible to Elsie,' I confess. 'She said something... about my parents, and I said she didn't have a dad.'

Cadence flinches.

'I didn't mean it. I'm really sorry.'

'Is that why she went on the course? She wasn't keen but then she suddenly changed her mind.'

I nod, ashamed.

'She didn't tell me any of this – which means she's protecting you too.'

I look at Grandma for reassurance. She gives me the smallest smile, but it's enough to hold me together. There's a long pause. I focus on the clock ticking.

'Sometimes people say things they shouldn't,' says Cadence quietly. 'Did Elsie make a comment about your parents and their trip to America?'

I'm frozen, but Cadence nods.

'That was insensitive of her but, ultimately, my fault. Your mum confided in me and I mentioned it to Elsie which I really shouldn't have done. I am very, very sorry.'

'*Everyone* is sorry,' says Grandma firmly.

So, it's *true?* Mum and Dad went to America to **TRY TO SAVE THEIR MARRIAGE?**

I turn to Grandma, panicked. 'Are they getting divorced? Don't they *love* one another anymore?'

'This is a chance for a fresh start for everyone,' says Grandma with quiet authority. '*Everyone,*' she stresses.

Like they have some sort of secret agreement, Cadence and Grandma stand up. If this was a question and answer session, well – it's over. Cadence hands me an envelope addressed to me in Elsie's handwriting.

'Elsie's home for a long weekend and she'll be glad to see you,' says Cadence. 'She's at the café.'

She pats my shoulder. I watch her leave, then slip into the garden and open the envelope.

Dear Ellie,

I'm sorry for the things I said too. Please forgive me.

Elsie x

Relief! I'm more like Eddie than I realised. I am not cut out for conflict. I find Juna and hand her Elsie's note. Juna was always the odd one out – the girl nobody quite wanted in their circle – and now she's the friend I can't do without.

'That's fair,' she says.

This is what Mum would call a 'life lesson.' No one is perfect. We all get things wrong, but we can apologise, forgive and move forward. I hope that's exactly what my parents are doing in America.

We get Herman and Tilly and head down to the Box Brownie Café. Elsie steps out just as Cooper and Jack emerge from the beach. It's obvious she's as nervous as me. Here's a shout-out for Herman – he's the BEST icebreaker. He adores Elsie and he's missed her. I defy anyone not to smile when there's a Labrador doing his happy pants dance.

'Hey Elsie!' calls Jack. 'Wanna hear what happened to poor old Cooper last night?'

'He's going to tell you whether you want him to or not,' says Cooper wryly.

'Scary stuff! *Very* scary stuff,' emphasizes Jack, having fun at Cooper's expense. *'Woo woo!'*

'I'm intrigued,' says Elsie.

The breeze shifts, pushing us closer together. Juna and I take Elsie's hands. We race down the slipway on to the beach, the boys in our slipstream howling ghoulishly. *Not scary!* Not in the light of day. Herman barks joyfully and Tilly, now part of our tribe, runs at our heels. We sprint to the edge of the cove, clamber over the rocks and pull ourselves onto the bank in front of the lighthouse. This is our go-to place. It's also where Elsie and I said hurtful things to each other. There's a moment of awkwardness as we sink into the grass.

'You don't need drama school, Elsie. We have shed loads of drama right here,' says Jack.

'Bella says the Little Egret is haunted and the hotel's been attacked–'

'Twice.'

'–in the *dead* of night–'

'With red paint which actually looked like blood.'

'–yeah – dripping down the wall.'

'They changed the sign from Little Egret to Bitter Regret.'

'Someone's threatening the Vittori family.'

Elsie's pretty horrified.

'Bella's dad banned photos – thought a hotel called Bitter Regret might put people off,' laughs Jack.

'I can see the logic in that,' says Elsie.

'And you'll never guess who's his–' I do bunny ears '– *"PR Consultant?"'* Dramatic pause. 'Gilby Flynn's dad!'

'Gilby's dad threatened Jack!'

'Told me to delete the photos I'd taken, or I'd *bitterly*

regret it,' says Jack.

Elsie gasps.

'But after all that secrecy, the story was in the Peregrine Post!'

'That's so weird,' says Juna.

'I can't leave you kids alone for two minutes before you fall headlong into trouble,' says Elsie, half laughing.

'That's not all. Cooper saw something strange last night on Portis Crag,' I say, with appropriate gravity. 'And before that, Eddie saw something too.'

'This is the woo woo bit,' says Jack in a – let's be honest – mocking tone.

I frown at him. He wasn't there. I *saw* how terrified Cooper was last night. Cooper explains what he *thinks* he saw and completely downplays it. Typical!

'Creepy. Maybe the hotel *is* haunted?' says Elsie.

'If it isn't, it soon will be. They're killing the Little Egret; too much bad publicity. Bella told me,' says Jack solemnly.

Put like that, it feels like the impending death of a living thing. Death is loss. Good things are lost – like the confidence I had in my parents and the love they had for each other. Suddenly, I have to blink back tears.

'What's going on?' Jack asks me, perplexed.

'Nothing,' I say. *Fleeting, shadowy thoughts.*

'The end of something is the beginning of something else,' says Cooper, gently.

He's trying to help me. I fall into his thought which flares for an instant, striking light in a fearful place. Cooper understands loss. His dad left home last Christmas and he hasn't seen him since. Reading between the lines, that was a decent outcome for Cooper and his mum – but my family is different. Isn't it?

Cooper digs in his pocket and pulls out the Little Egret keys.

'We should all have one to keep the memory of the Little Egret alive. That one's yours, Ellie,' says Cooper, giving me the key Eddie found on the beach.

'What's this? A secret society?' asks Jack.

'The Little Egret Friendship Society,' suggests Juna, accepting a key.

'Everyone who holds an egret key, will be a friend for life,' says Elsie, looking at me.

'I'm not sure I'm ready for this type of commitment,' says Jack, taking one anyway.

Elsie takes a key and there's peace between us. I take a deep breath. Truly special moments slip effortlessly into the past, though I'd freeze this one in time if I could. Keys free things from dark spaces where they can find the light and fly free. We clink our keys together.

Early hours. Almost awake.

Susannah, I know you need to be free. I understand. I do.

It's a huge thing for someone to commit to one person, even someone as good as Eddie. He's one of the very best people I will ever know – my own brother who has been hidden in plain sight my whole life – but he might not be the right one for you.

Susannah, you're important to me. We should say goodbye properly and wish one another luck. Shouldn't we? I want to thank you. You listened to me.

Susannah... You can fly away... You can find the light. You can be free...

Susannah...*

5:30 a.m. Kitchen. Eddie's laptop. Emailing…

Dear Mum and Dad,

I know you went to America to try to save your marriage. It's no one's fault that I know this. Please don't be angry.

I know you've got to do what's best for you. Every moment becomes history, so bad moments slip into the past, if we let them go. We might not forget them, but at least every day can be a fresh start. That's what Grandma says. Some things shouldn't slip away though. I've been thinking why people stop caring for one another. If love is something, won't it always be something? How can it become nothing? Let's make it a rule that, no matter what happens, we will always be a family who love one another. There's definitely more good in our family than bad.

Dad, you should be proud of Eddie. I know you were being sarcastic about giving Eddie pocket money, but if you did, he would probably give it to me. Grandma has always said Eddie is a giver, and it's true. Eddie told me I am imperfectly sound. That's true as well. I have not read the rule book. I'm sorry. I don't want an extra 50 rules in my life. I would never remember them all and I'd end up failing.

I love you both. And Fin. I love Eddie, though I think I've spent most of my life not realising it. I am glad I know it now. I'm glad Eddie and Fin are my brothers. I am glad you are my parents. You're the right ones for me.

Please don't forget, you loved one another once, and love, when it flies away, still exists somewhere.

Your loving daughter, Ellie xxx

Better late than never

We spend the afternoon on Susie Q. Eddie pilots the boat and the wind sweeps thoughts out of dark spaces for a while. I've not told anyone how I'm feeling but somehow, I feel understood. Juna puts her hand on my shoulder for no reason, and Cooper helps Eddie, learning the ropes to keep us all safe. From the sea the Little Egret's weathervane seems poised to take flight. Why should it stay when it's not wanted?

Later, at home, Eddie lights the barbeque. Everyone sprawls on our rickety benches and the solar lights in the magnolia tree begin to twinkle. I decide I will try to cast a bit of light into a life that might need it. I go inside and dial Abigail's number. Her dad answers the phone as if he's still on duty.

'Who is speaking, and what is the purpose of your call?'

'It's Ellie Booton. Is Abigail there, please?' I ask.

'And what is the purpose of your call?' he repeats.

'To speak to Abigail.'

'For what purpose?'

He makes me feel guilty when I've done nothing wrong. That's his special talent.

'We're having a barbeque. I wondered if Abigail would

like to come over.'

Awkward silence. I succumb to the pressure and start to ramble.

'Elsie's home for the weekend. Did you know she's doing a performing arts course?'

'A performing arts course?' he says, like it's a crime.

'We're having vegan sausages.'

'Vegan sausages? I've never *heard* of such a thing.'

'They're very tasty. We've got salad. We eat healthy stuff.'

'*Stuff?*' he splutters, disgusted.

This is torture. Finally, he gives the phone to Abigail. She's almost as hostile as her dad, and I can't go through *that* again.

'We're having a barbeque. Eddie's picking you up in five. Look out for him,' I tell her.

'OK,' she says, meekly, and hangs up.

Honestly, I've never felt so powerful in my *life!* I go into the garden and ask Eddie, politely, to drive to Abigail's house and bring her back. Everyone stares at me like I've fallen off my perch – then Eddie rights the situation by saying, 'No probs,' and Cooper, with a wry smile, takes over the tongs.

When Abigail arrives, we're dishing up. She gets out of Eddie's car looking confused and a bit scared, truth be told – but Juna, Elsie and I wave her over and Cooper slaps a plate of food in front of her and says, 'Get your chops around that.'

Herman, who has every right to hold a grudge, forgives Abigail the instant she has food and stares at her adoringly – and it's clear, Abigail's not used to being adored in any way, shape or form. She really could do with a dog in her life and a few lessons in kindness.

It all feels a bit strange at first. *Just be normal,* I tell myself. *I can reset this relationship, can't I? It will transform to become something else – though I'm not sure what.*

Grandma comes out of the house with a cushion and a gin and tonic and makes herself cosy on the swing. She chats to Herman, telling him about her day, which he's very interested in, and then she promises Herman sausage if he fetches his ball which, of course, he does. Abigail sits next to Jack and takes it all in. Yes, people talk to animals and animals understand and talk back in their own way. Cooper throws Herman's ball which becomes a game, with Herman high fiving anyone who will throw it for him. Eliza wanders outside with sleepy eyes and climbs on Grandma's lap. Tilly creeps out from under the bench and steals Herman's ball, so Herman pads into the house and comes out with another one. For the record, Herman is incapable of hard feelings.

'Come sailing with us, Grandma,' teases Eddie, knowing it will prompt Grandma to tell the story of her one and only voyage over the Irish Sea. It was a very rough crossing. If you're squeamish, hearing it for the first time can scar you for life, but it is funny and Abigail joins in the laughter. I guess Grandma will never be a sailor.

'Terra firma for me,' says Grandma. 'I'm not cut out for stormy seas.'

'Thanks for coming over,' I say to Abigail, when Eddie

fetches his car keys to run Elsie, Cooper and Abigail home.

'Whatever,' she says, and I almost laugh. Abigail has spent years practising the dark art of meanness and she's good at it. She may be influenced by her dad who likes to disapprove of everything that gives people pleasure.

'Good job, Ellie,' says Grandma, as we tidy up the garden. She hugs me and kisses my head. I'm not sure why I'm being praised, but I hold on to her and, for those moments, my family doesn't seem fragile at all.

Email from Mum.

My darling girl,

I read your email and cried. It's my job to protect you from any adult worry you have no control over, and I have failed. I am so sorry. Cadence phoned and explained how this came about. I understand she's apologised to you too. Thank you for writing this: *love, when it flies away, still exists somewhere*. It's an eloquent thought and something to ponder on. Please don't worry. Things will work out, one way or another.

Hope you're having sunny, carefree days. Give my love to Grandma and Eddie. Fin sends lots of kisses.

All my love, Mum xoxox

Email from Dad.

Dear Ellie,

It's awful being so far away because I want to give you a hug. Don't worry about your mum and me. Whatever happens in our lives, our family will always be our top priority. We knew Eddie would look after you. I am proud of him and I will tell him so. I am proud of you both. A barrel full of hugs and love. Stroke Eliza for me, give Herman a biscuit, and pour Grandma a gin and tonic. (Joking – make her a cup of tea.)

Your loving Dad xxx

P.S. Sorry the "All Alone and Abandoned" Rule Book, has been such a burden to you. It wasn't meant to be. We thought the title was funny and would pique your interest. Not to worry. Your rule has been easy to take to heart: *We are a family who will always love one another*. I agree, wholeheartedly, that *there's definitely more good in our family than bad*.

I read my parents' emails again. This is my family. This is life, stretched across time and space from before I was born, to after I will die. People with infinite choices and endless decisions which have consequences for the planet and every living thing on it. I will try to make good choices. I will hope for the best outcome.

I climb the stairs to my bedroom feeling gravity's force which fills a cavity in the middle of my chest. The *'All*

Alone and Abandoned' Rule Book has slipped and is now lodged, somewhere, under the bottom bunk behind dusty plastic boxes filled with stuff that might come in handy one day. I drag them out, which makes me sneeze, then I belly crawl under the bed. It's there. I grasp the envelope and wriggle out. I open the bottom drawer of my desk and place it inside. Then I gently close it. Now I don't have to read it, I probably will.

I find Eddie in the workshop.

'What's up, Chicken?' he says without looking up.

'Dad's emailed you,' I say.

Eddie sighs. 'I'll read it later.'

I stand in the doorway, watching. He's shaping the clay ears of a tumbling hare having the best day of its life, if only it were real. Somehow, Eddie knows how to capture joy. If only he could apply this skill to his own life.

'It might be a nice email. He might give you a compliment.'

'Unlikely,' says Eddie, sounding weary.

'He might.'

Eddie looks up. He washes and dries his hands, then picks up his smartphone. We look at one another expectantly. From the other side of the workbench, I watch his face. When he's finished reading, he slumps as though he's suddenly tired.

'What?' I ask.

Eddie needs a few moments to himself. He retreats to the far end of the workshop and looks out of the window. I read Dad's email to Eddie. It's apologetic and nice. So nice, in fact, that it is upsetting. Eddie is used to thinking of himself as a disappointment. Over the years, he's had a lot of criticism from a lot of people, except Grandma, who has always believed in him, however smelly, sad and scruffy he was.

If I hug him, I'll cry – so I pat him on the back and tell him how beautiful and funny the hare is, caught in a tangle of happy haste.

'He's late for a very important date,'* says Eddie.

'Dad's always been proud of you. Always. He didn't make it clear, that's all.'

'Better late than never.'

'Exactly,' I say.

'Thanks Ellie,' says Eddie, simply.

I am no longer the middle child with no clear role in life. I am Eddie's friend and ally.

Being there and listening

There's a polite knock on the front door. It's not anyone I expected. I manage to mash my surprise into a friendly smile. Abigail doesn't reciprocate. She follows me into the kitchen and makes a beeline for Jack.

Eddie stuffs a couple of notes into my hand. 'Buy your friends breakfast at the Box Brownie. My treat.'

There are definite advantages to having an older brother who earns money and keeps cash in his wallet. I hug him and he disappears into the workshop looking pleased. Jazz drifts into the kitchen. For once, Grandma is at her workbench and Eddie will have company today.

Juna jumps down the last three stairs, pulls on her trainers and we all step out together. Halfway down the hill, Cooper nudges me. Abigail's agitated. She once got into a bit of bother at the café and it's obvious she's not keen to return to the scene of a crime.*

Cooper shrugs. He's not quite over Abigail's dishonest tendencies. At the café entrance, Abigail separates from us.

'I'll wait outside,' she says, stiffly.

'No. You're with us,' I say. 'It's Eddie's treat.'

'Why should he treat me?' she asks. 'He doesn't even know me. Anyway, we're not friends.'

'Of course you're included,' I say and nudge Abigail into the café. I take a deep breath. Patience. Kindness. Hopefully we will find our way out of this troubled maze.

Elsie joins us and we all squeeze into a booth. The morning sun splashes the table and seagulls bounce on the roof, interrupting us with their raucous cries as we sort out who's having what. Abigail resists, so Elsie orders her a summer berry smoothie and blueberry pancakes.

'Trust me,' she says to Abigail. 'Mum's pancakes are special.'

Abigail begins to relax. There must be more to her than the pinched expression that masks her face every day. *How many rules does PC Jennings impose on his daughter?* I wonder. *More than fifty? Maybe Abigail and I have something in common after all?*

(Just letting you know – it's completely true. The pancakes are special.)

'If I could make pancakes like these, I would unravel the meaning of life,' Cooper calls to Cadence.

'Well, in that case, I'll give you the recipe,' she laughs.

'I overheard something...' says Abigail in the lull. 'If I tell you, you've got to promise you didn't hear it from me.'

'Sure,' I say. After all, I don't have to believe her.

'Someone phoned Dad last night to report something.'

'Was somebody having too much fun?' asks Cooper, a little unkindly.

Abigail looks at him coldly. 'Sure, if it's fun when someone sees a ghost.'

'No such thing,' says Jack flatly.

'I'm only telling you what was said. Forget it.'

122

We chew our food in silence.

'Where?' I ask.

'Where *what?*' snaps Abigail.

'Where was the, um, ghost seen?'

'On Portis Crag.'

'Is this for real? Did somebody tell you what happened to me?' asks Cooper, irritated.

Abigail colours slightly. 'I don't know what happened to you and I'm not lying,' she says.

It's awkward because we all know that Abigail's relationship with the truth is a tad unreliable. But here she is – a past enemy, telling us a story and wanting us to believe her.

'Eddie saw something strange a few nights ago,' I offer. I look at Cooper.

'OK,' he says reluctantly. 'I saw something strange too.'

Abigail seems relieved we're taking her seriously. Well, as far as anyone *can* take a ghost sighting seriously.

Jack pats Cooper on the shoulder. 'Oh man! No one's seen a ghost–'

'I never said I did.'

'–but maybe *something's* going on.'

'Well, that just about covers every possibility in the universe,' I say, annoyed with Jack for patronizing Cooper.

'You know what would be fun?' asks Jack.

'I'm sure you'll tell us,' I say.

'You want to photograph... whatever it is?' offers Juna.

Jack high fives her.

Why didn't I guess what Jack wanted to do? He's my friend too. I feel Cooper's eyes on me, and I'm not sure I know what he's thinking.

According to Jack, there's only one thing to do, apparently. Check it out. We set off along the beach, scramble over the rocks at the end of the cove, skirt the cornfield and climb over the stile. We follow the track along Portis Crag.

'This is where it was,' says Abigail.

'Here?' asks Juna.

'Well, roughly, yeah.'

'Who saw it?'

'How should I know? I only heard Dad's side of the conversation.'

'Well, what did they see, exactly?' asks Cooper.

'I've *told* you. A *ghost*. Last night. Here. Didn't you hear me the first time?'

We're at the point where the track forks – one side descending to the harbour, the other joining the Coast Road which runs past the Little Egret.

'Are you thinking what I'm thinking?' Jack asks generally.

'I doubt it,' says Cooper.

'Eden,' Jack says. 'I bet it's Eden.'

'Nah,' says Cooper – but Jack's on a roll and takes charge of this expedition. I have a feeling that he needs an excuse to see Bella.

When the hotel comes into sight, it's obvious things are happening. Closed circuit cameras have been fixed to the wall and there are workers in overalls milling about. A man on a ladder is trying to remove the 3D letters of the hotel sign. The L from LITTLE is cockeyed but, otherwise, still firmly attached.

"ells bells. There's no way I can get these off with a spanner,' he complains, puffing and sweating.

Mr Vittori stands guard. 'Try harder, man!' he commands.

'I could belt it with a lump 'ammer. Would you like me to try that, Mr Vittori?'

'No! I want you to do what I asked: remove the letters, carefully and quickly.'

'I can't! I'll 'ave to cut 'em off with an angle grinder. And I'll need an 'oist. They're as 'eavy as lead.'

This is turning into a show. Spanner-man's huge bottom wobbles as he descends the ladder.

'This won't do! Get back up that ladder! The L is crooked,' yells Mr Vittori, obsessing.

'Excitable little twonk, isn't he?' whispers Cooper.

'It was a crook who fixed 'em. The 'ole 'otel might fall down if I remove them bolts. They'd 'old an ocean liner together,' says Spanner-man cheerfully.

Minus his wobbly bottom, I think I quite like him. Mr Vittori fumes and stomps off, giving Jack the chance to take a few defiant photographs.

'Why change its name anyway?' mutters Spanner-man. 'What's wrong with the Little Egret? It's got an 'istory this place. Oi, you're a strappin' lad,' he says, noticing Jack. "elp me with these ladders, will you?'

Spanner-man collapses the ladder and Jack helps to tilt and carry it to a van. The gravel is messed up, so Cooper and I smooth it with our feet.

'Where's your dog? Has it pooped?' asks Eden,

appearing like a toxic pixie.

'Grief, Eden,' I say, exasperated. 'What's wrong with hello?'

'So, why are you here?' he asks.

'You'd think, growing up in the hospitality business, you'd be a bit more hospitable,' says Cooper.

'Like father, like son,' says Jack dryly, slapping dust off his hands.

I see Cooper flinch. Comparing sons to their fathers is sometimes not a compliment. Not in Eden's case, and not in Cooper's either.

'Jack!'

We look up. Bella appears at her bedroom window. A minute later, her dazzling self materializes in front of us.

'I didn't know you were coming to see me,' she says, delighted.

'We're starting to join the dots of your ghost story,' says Jack.

'I'm all ears,' she says, flashing a mean smile at me.

I pull my hair over my ears.

Jack does the talking – not Cooper, who *actually* saw the ghost-not-ghost.

'Is your sweet little brother fond of dressing up?' Jack asks Bella.

'Pardon?'

'And going woo-woo, woo-woo?' he says, mimicking a cartoon ghost.

'You're not listening, Jack. I was there and it wasn't Eden,' says Cooper.

'Gilby's unhinged, but Jack's a nutter,' says Eden

disgusted, and walks off.

Jack is undeterred. He lights up when he talks to Bella, and she is so busy flicking her hair and batting her eyelashes that she doesn't notice me and my ears sneak away. I find Eden alone in the garden, listlessly pulling the heads off roses.

'Don't do that!' I say. 'Your dad will go ape.'

'How will he know?'

'Because, you dope, that CCTV camera can see you.'

Eden is shocked and scared, which tells me a lot about his relationship with his father.

'Besides, what did those roses ever do to you?'

'What do you want?' he asks, rudely.

'Um. You said Gilby was unhinged. Why did you say that?'

He ignores my question. 'Tell me about the ghost,' he says.

I tell him about Cooper's experience.

'Could be anything,' says Eden. 'A plastic bag caught on a twig.'

'True,' I say.

We study one another. He's not a bad kid – just lonely and bored with some unfortunate spiteful tendencies that he's probably been taught by example. I know a bit about loneliness myself, though it never induced me to decapitate roses.

'I can see everything from up there,' he says, waving his hand vaguely at the hotel. 'I'll keep a lookout.'

'Only if you have time and it's safe,' I say.

'I'll text you if I see something.'

'Text Cooper. I don't have a mobile.'

He sniggers and prepares to insult me.

'Don't say anything,' I warn him. 'We were just starting to get along.'

'Wanna know why Gilby's unhinged? He likes my sister!'

Wow. Brotherly love.

'And he cries when he thinks no one's looking.'

I don't know what to say. I walk back to find the others. Jack and Bella are still performing their double act. Elsie discreetly rolls her eyes.

I look at my watch. 'We should go,' I say.

'I'll hang for a while,' says Jack casually, smiling at Bella.

Abigail's expression is pinched again. She's defeated. Jack's not interested in her – at all. She picks up her bag and follows us out.

'Bye Jack,' I call but he's already forgotten we were there. 'So much for our Friendship Society,' I mutter under my breath.

'Friendship society? How dumb is that?' says Abigail, unpleasantly.

Abigail wearies me. 'It's not dumb for people who value friends,' I say.

I suggest going down to the boat. We can sit and bob on the water for a while, but Abigail's not interested. We part company at the top of Portis Crag, and she walks off with no clear plan for her day. If she's lonely, this is not the best way to combat it, but these are her choices.

***

Cooper emerges from the cabin. 'No biscuits left,' he says sadly.

We sit in the sunshine not talking.

'Is that Eden?' says Juna, noticing a boy at the edge of the jetty. 'He's followed us down here.'

Eden looks forlorn, the male equivalent of Orphan Annie.

'That kid's a mess,' says Cooper, knowingly. He waves and shouts, 'Hey, Eden!'

Eden saunters over and climbs on the boat.

'Would you like a drink?' asks Cooper. 'No biscuits, I'm afraid.'

'You only had crumby digestives anyway. Can't you get chocolatey ones?' says Eden.

'Have you been on Eddie's boat when we're not here?' I ask, shocked.

'It wasn't locked,' he says, without shame.

'You are an entitled little–'

I cut Cooper off. That wasn't going to be a compliment. 'Tell Cooper what you told me,' I command.

'What? That the ghost is a plastic bag caught on a twig?' mocks Eden.

'About keeping a lookout at night,' I say. This kid wears me out.

'Sure. I could do that if I don't have something more important to do – which is *always*,' he says – then, 'This is boring.' He climbs off the boat, calling over his shoulder, 'Good luck with your stupid ghost.'

He strolls down the jetty, hands in pockets.

'Thanks for gracing us with your presence,' calls

Cooper.

'Is it just me, or is that kid hard to like?' asks Elsie.

'He told me he'd seen Gilby crying.' I tell her about the row Gilby had with his dad and how Gilby collapsed in the cornfield and hobbled away, sobbing.

Elsie shakes her head, incredulous. 'Wow. I always had the idea that Gilby's life was golden.'

'Apparently not,' says Cooper, whose own life is complicated and worrying – not golden at all.

'*All that glisters is not gold.* Someone told me that was Shakespeare,' I tell Cooper, who smiles. It's my way of telling him, I'm there and I listen.

The key to survival

Susannah answers on the tenth ring. I really want to talk to her.

'Hi Ellie,' she says. 'Are you OK?'

'I think so,' I say. 'Are you?'

'I'm OK. Are you having fun with Elsie?'

'Elsie's away on a performing arts course for the summer. She was home for the weekend though.'

'Oh. Are you missing her?'

'I've got used to it. Juna's staying with me.'

'You're not lonely then,' says Susannah, sounding lonely. 'How's Cooper?'

'He's OK.'

'How's Jack?'

'He's OK too.'

'I guess we're all OK.'

It's true that people say they're OK when sometimes, they're not. That's one thing adults teach kids by example, and I'm not sure it's a good thing. I listen to the silence between us. I've started to forget how easy it was to talk to her. It seems much harder now.

Out of nowhere I ask, 'Do you believe in the saying, *Like father, like son?*'

'We might be influenced by certain people but, in the end, we make our own choices. Eddie's not a clone of your dad, is he?'

'No. There's no one quite like Eddie,' I say.

'That's true,' says Susannah.

I can't tell if she's missing him. Another silence.

'Do you still like Susie Q?' she asks.

'She's great. I love her,' I say thinking, *what's not to like about a boat?*

'And does Eddie... like her?'

'He loves her too.'

'That's good,' says Susannah, sounding very sad. 'Well, goodbye, Ellie. It was nice talking to you.'

'Bye,' I say, feeling empty. I'm not sure I can do this again.

The doorbell rings. Who could possibly make my morning bleaker? Gilby? Abigail? I open the door. It's worse. It's Alfred.

'Are you here to see Grandma? Would you like to come in?' I say, with due respect to my polite upbringing.

'Thank you, Ellie,' says Alfred, mistaking it for friendliness. 'How lovely to see you. Isn't it a beautiful morning?'

Grandma must be a sucker for old fashioned charm, and I suspect Alfred ladles it out like soup.

'These are for you, my dear,' he says, presenting me with a bunch of yellow tulips.

Never before, in my *entire* life, have I been given flowers. I never imagined my first bunch would be from an old man with a grandma crush. I step back and shudder.

'Thank you,' I choke. 'Come in.'

Grandma floats down the stairs and into his arms. He gives her a smacker on the cheek. They drift into the garden and I spy on them through the kitchen window. He must be a joker because Grandma can't stop laughing. *Sickening*.

Cooper jogs up the hill and vaults over the gate, stopping to have a word with Grandma and Alfred. Now *he's* laughing. He high fives Alfred. *What* is happening? My friends are betraying me. I go into the den and close the door. Five minutes later Cooper looks in.

'What are you doing?' he asks. 'I've been calling you.'

'I didn't hear,' I lie, wrapped in the gloom of a dark mood.

Cooper sits opposite me, making it almost impossible to avoid eye contact. He says one word: 'Explain.'

He's not asking for a breakdown of Pythagoras' theorem, or an answer to, *Why did the chicken cross the road?* and he's prepared to wait...

'It's Susannah,' I say, eventually. 'And Grandma... And my parents.' I try to shake the thoughts from my head, but they're stuck. There's a lump in my throat and I would be *mortified* to cry in front of him.

'Don't fight what you can't change, Ellie.'

I say nothing.

'Seriously. Be careful. Always hope for the best outcome. It's the key to survival.'

This is a crossroads. This is where I make a choice. There are several paths I could follow – one descends steeply to a light deprived place. Cooper knows what he's talking about. He has faced things in his life I might never face in mine. Not trusting my voice, I nod and stand up. *Be optimistic,* I think. *Hope for the best outcome.*

Cooper throws a few bendy dance shapes. Ha ha. Very funny. Against my will, a smile breaks through. Cooper is my *most* annoying friend.

'OK. Now can I tell you something that might really tick you off? Forget the Little Egret friendship pledge we made. Gilby's old man collared Jack yesterday and told *him* to tell *me* that Mr Vittori wants the keys back. Said Bella got it wrong telling us we could keep them.'

'I thought they were worthless?'

'They are. He just doesn't want us to have them. Jack's already surrendered his.'

'I'm not sure he deserved one in the first place,' I say.

We're in the garden with Grandma and *Alfred.* Alfred tells us he overheard a conversation between Mr Vittori and Liam Flynn, and the big secret is this: The Little Egret hotel is to be renamed – wait for it – *Sea View.* A hotel with a sea view called, Sea View. They must have struggled to come up with that one.

'That's the best they could do?' I say, unable to resist getting involved in the conversation.

'It will always be the Little Egret to me,' says Grandma. 'The egret weathervane is a local landmark.'

'That's going too,' says Alfred.

'Good grief. Why do people need to change what already works?'

'*Exactly* Grandma,' I say forcefully – thinking that

Grandma's interest in Alfred is a new thing I shouldn't have to get used to.

I shoot a dirty look at Alfred who, thank goodness, doesn't see. Pants! This *hope for the best* lark is harder in practice.

'Sea View,' muses Alfred. 'Obvious. Boring. Banal. Disappointing considering the hotel's history.'

'What's that?' asks Juna.

'Some parts of the hotel date back to the eighteenth century. The place was a veritable haven for smugglers. All sorts of contraband: brandy, tea, tobacco.'

'You seem to know a lot about it,' I say, in an offhand way.

'I enjoy tales of tax dodging. I'm a retired tax inspector,' says Alfred with a twinkle in his eye.

'*A tax inspector?*' I say, appalled. 'I thought you had an *interesting* job.'

Grandma zaps me with her eyes and I am duly warned. Grandma would never be rude to one of my friends.

Alfred is kinder than I deserve. 'It was exciting, Ellie. What some people will do to avoid paying their fair whack of tax!' he says, ruefully. 'Nothing is certain in life except death and taxes.'* He sighs. 'Now I'm an old boy, and not much use to anyone.'

Grandma is old and the least useless person I know. Old people are usually closer to death than younger ones. I've already lost Grandpa. I must cherish Grandma every day and try to make her happy. My resistance to Alfred begins to crumble.

'Are you single?' I ask him.

Grandma gasps, but Alfred doesn't flinch. 'My wife died seven years ago. She was called Katy. A wonderful, funny, feisty woman. I miss her every day. I'm alone, so yes, I'm single.'

You've got to appreciate an adult who gives a direct answer. 'Grandma is funny... And feisty,' I add, unsure of what feisty means.

'Your grandmother is certainly funny and feisty,' he says, reaching for Grandma's hand and giving it a squeeze. 'And completely wonderful, as you already know.'

'I do know that. She's my grandma.'

Children might not be clones of their parents, but I want to be a bit like Grandma, who is everything that is strong and spirited, wise and good. Grandma likes Alfred, so I will do my best to like him too.

It's lunchtime. I'm hungry and feeling a whole heap better. I flash Cooper a comical grin. My choice is that it's not going to be a dark day after all. We make sandwiches and eat them in the garden. Cooper's already shown Alfred his key, which Alfred thinks is practically worthless – probably made of brass – though a lot of brass fixtures and fittings could be recycled for a decent wad of cash. I ask if the Little Egret's weathervane is made of brass.

'It's burnished copper. I read that in the Peregrine Post. The novelty of it will be worth something though. I wonder if he'll declare *that* on his tax return?' says Alfred, then, 'Apologies. I am no longer employed by HMRC* and it's not my business. My bad!' which makes us laugh.

I quiz Alfred on Bella's ghost story. Had he heard any mysterious bumps in the night? No, he says, but wouldn't it be something if he did bump into a ghost one night! Wasn't there something about a ghost in the news article? As for the Bitter Regret attack, he thinks that's plain weird and a bit sinister.

'Someone's obviously out to cause him bother, poor fella,' says Alfred, 'though he bought a hotel so he's not all that poor, is he?'

Alfred's not a fan of Mr Vittori who, he says, reminds him of a puffed-up peacock with a few loose bum feathers.

Grandma thinks this comment is somewhat inappropriate, considering that children tend to repeat what grown-ups say, and Alfred apologises. I think it's funny and a fair appraisal, considering what we know about Mr Vittori. I think I quite like Alfred. What a difference a day makes.

Juna, Cooper and I wade into the sea in our shorts. Cooper takes a selfie of us with the Little Egret hotel behind us in the distance. He sends it to Elsie with a text:

Keep your egret key safe coz a peacock with loose bum feathers wants it back.

'I'm not rushing up there to hand the keys back,' says Cooper defiantly. 'Vittori can stuff it.'

A room with a view

Juna's gone home to see her mum and I am committed to spending the evening with Grandma and Alfred. I'm wearing a dress because Grandma asked me to. She's gone ahead and Cooper and Eddie are waiting for me in the kitchen. Feeling self-conscious, I go downstairs.

Eddie smiles. He doesn't comment on my appearance because he knows I would be embarrassed. I can't help commenting on how Cooper looks though. He's wearing a shirt and tie and he's had his hair cut.

'Boss!' I say.

'I know,' says Cooper, sheepishly, running his fingers through his hair. 'Your grandma has more influence than Mahatma Gandhi... You look nice.'

Compliments. I have never known what to do with them.

'Who could climb a tree in this?' I say.

'Do you need to climb a tree?' asks Cooper.

'I might.'

Cooper laughs, and we're back to our usual selves. I'm Ellie, with a smudge of lip gloss, and he's Cooper, wearing a tie.

'Come on,' says Eddie. 'Your carriage awaits.'

***

We clink our glasses together. The Little Egret restaurant (open to non-residents) is pretty cool. My parents are in America trying to get their act together and Eddie and I are here, chaperoning our grandmother with her new boyfriend. Alfred is quite funny for an old retired bloke, and Grandma seems very happy. I have reached a point of peace and understanding with my brother – though that's probably what he offered all along – I just couldn't see it. And somehow, Cooper, who was in enemy territory when I first met him, has become an extra in my family. Susannah, who I thought was one of us, has gone. The ebb and flow of life – and somehow, we survive it.

We're having a lovely time. There are vegan choices for Eddie, and once you discover mocktails, you can't have just one. Through the plate glass wall, I see Gilby Flynn's dad enter the lobby and, worse, he sees me. The way he looks at me makes me feel... uncomfortable. Eden appears on the other side of a potted palm. Liam Flynn speaks to him and Eden stabs his finger in my direction. Ten seconds later, Liam Flynn towers over our table.

'Excuse me,' he says, with a fake smile.

Grandma and Albert look up. They smile too, but my face is frozen. Let me tell you something. In life there are *red flags*. Dad talks about red flags when he feels something, or someone, is bad news – like the politician he wrote about who turned out to be, in Dad's words: '*A narcissistic twit who lies when the truth would do, and would trade his own granny for bubble gum.*' Red flags are warnings you feel in your gut, even when you've just stuffed your face with hot fudge cake.

'Sorry to interrupt your evening. May I have a word with this young man?' says Liam, singling out Cooper.

'I don't think we've been introduced,' says Eddie, politely.

'Liam Flynn, PR Consultant to Mr Vittori, owner of this establishment,' he says, not looking at Eddie. 'Cooper, isn't it? You're the boy who found the Egret key.'

Cooper looks at him uncertainly.

'The hotel stopped using keys a while ago, so... *where* did you find it?' he asks, with a hint of menace.

Eddie steps in. 'I found it on the beach by the rocks near the edge of the cove.'

'And *you* are?' asks Liam rudely.

'Eddie Booton, a paying customer.'

Eddie doesn't like this guy, I can tell. Good instincts, Eddie.

'*When* did you find the key?' presses Liam.

It was the day after Susannah left and Eddie was in a bad way.

'Bella may have dropped it,' I offer. 'She was on the beach with Gilby the day before.'

'Gilby?' He's not smiling now.

'That's right. Your son.'

He barely looks at me, switching his attention back to Cooper. 'That key, and the other keys you *helped* yourself to, must be returned,' he says curtly. 'How many did you take?'

Cooper swallows. 'Five, including the one Eddie found. Jack has already given his key to you.'

'Let's be clear,' says Liam Flynn, all pretence of

friendliness gone, 'it was never *his* key.' He leans into Cooper. 'Please return the other keys to me tomorrow. Do you understand?'

'Cooper only has one. I have the one Eddie found on the beach. We've given the others to friends,' I tell him.

Eddie stands up. 'I'll request them,' he says mildly. 'Then I'll liaise directly with Mr Vittori, the owner of this establishment.'

Liam looks like he could spit nails. 'Of course,' he says. Then to Grandma and Alfred: 'Enjoy the rest of your evening.' Big fake smile. And *exit.*

'He's not getting his grubby mitts on them,' says Eddie.

'Why did that feel so creepy?' asks Grandma, flustered.

'Probably because the guy's a total creep,' says Alfred. 'He's no business ordering other people's kids around. Cheeky sod! Sorry, Ruby. I know. *Language.* Are you OK?' he asks Cooper and me.

When we've all calmed down and I've drained the last dregs of my *Very Berry Bouquet* mocktail, Cooper and I say thank you and wander out to stretch our legs. On a coffee table in reception is a copy of the Peregrine Post with its headline article on the Bitter Regret attacks. I look at it, wondering why, when they tried to hush it up, the story ended up in print and on the Internet. As usual, Eden is curled up in the corner by the window, with a Nintendo. Cooper gives him a gentle nudge.

'You look weird,' he says to Cooper.

'Thanks,' says Cooper, straightening his tie. 'That's what I was going for.'

Eden appraises me. 'You look... nice. Not five stars nice,'

he adds, qualifying his compliment. 'What are you doing here? Bella doesn't like you.'

Cooper and I exchange a look which says: *the feeling is mutual.* 'We've just had dinner in the restaurant,' I say, 'as you well know. What did Liam Flynn say to you when you pointed us out?'

'He wanted to know–' he looks at Cooper '–if you were the one who stole our keys.'

Cooper nearly chokes. 'I didn't *steal* anything!'

Eden shrugs. 'Wanna see my room? You won't bump into my dad. He's not here tonight.'

I sigh. 'Sure.'

We follow him through a door marked *Private.* We go up a narrow staircase and along a corridor. Eden's bedroom is small, a bit drab, though tidily stuffed with books and technology. I kneel on his bed to look out of the window. Branches of an oak tree make the room gloomy and partially obstruct the view. He's definitely oversold it as a lookout post.

'Great room,' says Cooper. It's not, but Cooper is kind. 'Have you seen anything?' he asks, nodding towards the window.

'What like? A tweetie bird in a t-wee? I can't see anything out of that window, idiot. Follow me!'

He runs off and we have to chase him to keep up. More stairs, down a corridor, through a heavy wooden door which opens into – wow! – a room with a view. Another door leads out onto the roof where the egret weathervane is fixed.

'I can see everything from up here. I can see your

house–' the rooftop of my home is just visible on the other side of the cove '–and I know when you're on that wreck you call a boat.'

'Honestly, Eden, if you could dial down the insults, we might get along,' I say.

'I'm like my dad,' says Eden. 'That's what people say, anyway.'

I'm not sure what to say. I really don't like his dad and Eden is mostly a pain in the butt.

'Well, that's your choice,' says Cooper, quietly. 'But I'm nothing like mine.'

Eden looks at Cooper with interest. I don't need to say anything in response to Cooper's remark. Cooper, in the end, makes good choices. He is trusted in my family.

It's twilight. The temperature drops, and I shiver. The sea is hazy – a sea fret is closing in and the weathervane creaks as the wind picks up. In these conditions, it would be easy to imagine a wisp of something hovering on the cliff top.

Life threatening choices

It's a glorious morning. Herman trots on ahead. He knows we're on our way to meet Juna and Cooper and he stops at the top of the harbour road to wait for me. Tilly is on a lead – she's distracted and pulling. Last night she was agitated and climbed onto the window seat and howled at the darkness. We're the first to arrive. I sit down on the wall and wait. Below, the harbour is deserted and the air shimmers with heat.

Herman sniffs, stands up and wags his tail expectantly, even before Juna and Cooper come into sight. I wave, glad to see them. We make our way down the cobbles, along the jetty and climb aboard Susie Q, our new go-to place to hang out. I unpack the picnic in the galley. Cooper's brought fruit and chilled water, and Juna's got a bag of fresh clothes. We settle ourselves on the deck, happily munching apples.

'How was Alfred last night?' asks Juna.

'He was OK,' I say, keeping my voice neutral.

Cooper laughs. 'Ellie's about to start a fan club for Alfred. He called Liam Flynn a creep.'

'A *total* creep,' I correct him.

'What happened?'

We tell Juna how Liam Flynn ordered us to return the

Egret keys today.

'What's it got to do with Liam Flynn, anyway? The keys don't belong to him!' says Juna, indignant.

'Exactly,' I say. 'We'll wait until Elsie comes home, then we'll give the keys back to Mr Vittori.'

I look up at the Little Egret hotel, perched on the cliff above us. I can identify the lookout post, to the left of the little egret weathervane. I wonder if Eden is there now, looking down on people getting on with their lives. *Looking down* – that's just what he does – with his insults and his star ratings. Why does he do that, I wonder?

Herman alerts us to Jack coming down the jetty. He waves cheerfully, and my heart sinks. If relationships are mocktails, I might be strawberry, and Jack is... celery. We don't quite blend.

It's not long before Jack asserts himself. He wants to walk along the cliffs to the high point called Crangle Pass, so we leave the boat, climb the steep harbour road and join the coastal path. Juna and Cooper have walked this way before, but it's new to me and Jack. There's a sign: **WARNING! DANGEROUS CLIFFS. SHEER DROP BELOW. RISK OF DEATH. KEEP AWAY FROM THE EDGE!**

We don't deviate from the well-worn path. On the land side, wheat fields ripple in the breeze giving the impression they're alive and breathing together. We climb steadily, our ascent giving a view of our cove and the jagged coastline beyond in either direction. Over the sea, seagulls and cormorants glide, dipping out of sight below us, their cries mixed with the sound of surf smashing against the cliff face.

Cooper hands me a bottle of chilled water and I'm grateful. It's hot and I sink into the grass. He cups his hands and I pour water for Herman and Tilly who drink, thirstily.

'Sunrise would be incredible to photograph from up here,' says Jack.

'You'd have to get here before sunrise,' says Cooper. 'That would be dangerous.'

'I like a challenge,' says Jack.

'Yeah, but not a life threatening one,' says Cooper.

'I could get here before sunset and camp overnight.'

'What, all by yourself?'

'Sure. Why not? It's warm. All I'd need is a sleeping bag.'

I imagine being here, alone – the fields whispering strange secrets on the night breeze; the waves beating the rocks below.

'Well, good luck with that,' I say.

'What about you, Cooper? Want to join me?' asks Jack. 'Or are you still hung up on ghosts and ghouls?'

'Don't quite fancy crawly critters in my ears,' says Cooper, and I notice him shudder despite the warm wind.

'Nah,' says Jack, 'it's the ghosts you're afraid of.'

On the way back, we join the Coast Road and keep to the shady side. We've drunk all the water and it's too hot to talk. We're almost at the point where we climb over the stile to take the shortcut through the cornfield. A car roars past, brakes aggressively and is jammed into reverse, skidding to a stop beside us in a cloud of dust. I yank Tilly's lead, pulling her onto the grass verge. I'm only slightly less frightened to see it's Liam Flynn and not a total stranger. Gilby's in the passenger seat. The window's down and if I reached out, I could touch him. Herman senses tension – his hackles rise, and he gives a warning bark.

Liam Flynn leans over his son to spit words at us.

'You!' he says to me. 'Have you got the key?'

It's in my pocket.

'Hand it over!'

I'm not sure I can speak. The silence shimmers like heat. I see the shocked faces of Cooper and Jack. I look into the car. Gilby's attention is fixed on something far away. He swallows and blinks and I get the feeling he's trapped.

Juna steps forward. 'Leave us alone or we'll call the police!' she says with authority. She grabs my wrist, pulling me away from the car and across the road. 'Come on!' she urges the others.

We clamber over the stile and I stumble and graze my knee. We hurry on, checking we're not being followed.

'What's *wrong* with that guy?' asks Cooper.

No one has an answer. We're too rattled to make conversation. At the junction of Curly Lane, Jack shrugs and plods off towards town where his Auntie Maggie lives.

'I have to go too,' says Cooper. He helps his mum do their supermarket shop. 'You did great, Juna,' he says, putting his arm around her.

'Really great,' I say, joining in the hug.

We stand together for a few seconds, grateful for the closeness.

'Leave us alone or we'll call the police!' I command, imitating Juna.

'Cop Jennings to the rescue! Brace yourselves for a dose of disapproval.'

We laugh, relaxing a little.

'I've got the key with me,' I say, pulling it from my pocket and not feeling in the least bit guilty I didn't hand it over.

'Take mine, Ellie,' says Cooper, handing me his key. 'You can be the keeper of keys.'

'The Little Egret Friendship Society will still exist without them,' says Juna, giving me hers.

We part ways with Cooper. Juna and I head home. Herman and Tilly are panting. It was wrong to take them to Crangle Pass in the heat. I shouldn't have followed Jack. I need to make better choices. We climb the hill – hot, bothered and hungry. The day hasn't quite gone to plan, and the picnic and Juna's bag are still on the boat.

Grandma sits under the magnolia tree with Alfred. It feels wrong to spoil their relaxed mood, so we don't disturb them. The workshop is empty, and Eddie's car isn't on the drive. That gives me time to think, because I'm pretty sure there will be consequences when I tell Eddie and Grandma what happened this afternoon.

Liam Flynn's expression is burned on my brain. Liam Flynn is an angry man. Something he said really bothers me: **You!** *Have* **you** *got the key?* I was singled out and I don't know why.

Juna's having a shower. I change into light cotton shorts and flop down on the window seat. I place the keys down, side by side. The decorative bow of the keys are slightly different, and the bits that go into the lock are cut into different shapes, obviously, because they're made to lock different doors.

The doorbell rings. Liam Flynn's car is parked on the road and Gilby is at the door. Grandma and Alfred are still in the garden, in a world of their own. They might even be snoozing. Gilby looks back at the car and I see his dad gesture aggressively. Gilby rings the bell again. Then he looks up and sees... me.

I go downstairs, put the chain on and crack the door open a few inches to face the boy who made my life a misery: Gilby, the bully, who hurts people.

'I've come for the key,' he says, not looking at me.

I can see his dad from this angle – practically hanging out of the car to watch us, and I feel under threat. I wish Eddie was here.

Gilby shifts uncomfortably, glances back at his dad, then he says something completely unexpected: 'Tell me to go away.'

Still no eye contact. I feel my heart thumping.

'I'll go and get my grandma,' I say, uncertainly.

'Tell me to go away and I'll go.'

'OK. Go away.'

It's strange saying something so impolite to someone – even someone like Gilby.

Gilby stands his ground for the longest minute of my life. His father watches his back. Then his arms flail, as

149

though he's frustrated or angry, and he turns and strides down the path to his dad's car.

'I tried!' I hear him yell. He leaps in the car and it jets off with no regard for the speed limit.

Juna, dressed after her shower, leans over the bannister.

'What on earth was *that?*' she asks.

'Something really, really weird,' I say.

At six o'clock, Eddie drives up the hill with Cooper.

'Overnight guest,' says Eddie, opening the boot and unloading shopping. 'Bumped into Cooper and his mum in the supermarket. She got a text offering her a night shift, so Cooper's bunking down here for the night.'

'I can stay at home by myself,' says Cooper, defensively, though I can tell he's glad of the company.

We help Eddie with the shopping and Cooper, without being asked, takes the frozen food to the freezer and packs it away.

'You've been gone ages,' I say to Eddie. Something in my tone makes Eddie pause.

'What's happened?' he asks.

We eat salad in the kitchen with the windows and doors open. The heat is stifling. Grandma, Alfred and Eddie pay attention to our story. Grandma is outraged that *anyone* would approach children the way Liam Flynn approached us, and how could *any* parent use their own child as a weapon of intimidation, the way Liam used Gilby to knock on the door and ask for the key?

'Tell me to go away,' says Grandma echoing Gilby. 'What's going on in that boy's head?'

Eddie thinks we should call the police. Alfred is quiet and then he asks to see the keys.

I grab them from the window seat and race downstairs, setting them neatly on the table in front of Alfred. They're all clean and brightly polished.

'What is the key to the keys?' mulls Alfred, perching his glasses on the end of his nose. 'As Shakespeare might say, *To key or not to key. That is the question.*'

'Hamlet. Act 3, Scene 1,' says Cooper who reads Shakespeare without being ordered to.

'Impressive,' says Alfred, complimenting Cooper. 'Something motivates this Flynn character. What could it be?'

We stare at the keys as though they'll start explaining themselves.

'I noticed something,' I say. 'The key that Eddie found feels heavier.'

I point it out. Alfred picks it up and weighs it in his hand. Then he sniffs it. How odd. He weighs the other keys and sniffs them too.

'They're brass,' he says. 'But this one –' he picks out the heavy key '– is different.'

'Gold is heavier than brass and doesn't smell of anything,' says Cooper.

Are you serious? How does Cooper know this stuff?

'Exactly. There's no odour,' says Alfred. 'I think this one may be gold.'

We look at it in stunned silence.

'Liam Flynn has stumbled across treasure,' says Grandma. 'No wonder he wants it back.'

'Well, it's not worth a fortune. Unless, of course, there are more of them.'

'We need to tell someone about this,' says Eddie. 'Vittori, or the police. The whole thing is shady. I don't want him coming back here or harassing the kids.'

'Let's sleep on it,' says Grandma. 'We'll make a decision in the morning.'

It's twilight. Cooper, Juna and I squash together on the creaky garden swing. The wind is picking up and there's an army of clouds gathering over the sea. We've texted Elsie to tell her about the day's developments, though Grandma has warned us not to jump to conclusions about the golden key. *Maybe he was trying to recover it for Mr Vittori?* said Grandma, though she didn't sound convinced.

'Remember the number that was flipped on the guest room door?'

'Room twenty-nine?'

'I'll bet Liam Flynn unscrewed the numbers, saw they were brass, and screwed the nine back on, upside down by mistake. He's systematically going through the hotel searching for gold.'

The thought of Liam Flynn, haunting the Little Egret in the middle of the night, is pretty disturbing.

'If Gilby wanted the key for his dad, why did he tell me to send him away? It doesn't make sense.'

***

The first thing I'm aware of is Herman sniffing deeply by the door. He's not a spring chicken. He may need to go out to pee. I swing my legs out of the top bunk and lower myself gently down. Juna is fast asleep. Tilly isn't. She's on the window seat, alert, staring into the darkness. A huge clap of thunder rattles the windows. Tilly flattens her body and whimpers. A storm is raging over the sea.

There's a tap on my door. In a muffled whisper I hear, 'Ellie? Are you awake?' It's Cooper, dressed and dishevelled.

We creep downstairs and I unlock the door to let Herman go into the garden.

'Jack's just texted me. He went to Crangle Pass last night. He's up there in this storm.'

'Oh, good grief. Doesn't that boy check the weather forecast?' I say wearily, sounding like my dad.

'The wind's strong. He's no flashlight so he can't get down.'

Lightning forks across the sky, followed by thunder. And then it starts to rain. Hard.

'And now he'll get soaked. What a twonk.' I say, irritated. 'Watch out for Herman. I'll go and ask Eddie what we should do.'

My parents always complained that my brother was so good at switching off and checking out, he could sleep for a week on a clothesline. Not anymore. He's awake. Maybe it's the worry of having a younger sister to look out for?

'Eddie?'

'What?'

'Jack's camping on Crangle Pass and he's texted Cooper.

There's a storm and he's stuck up there.'

I won't write down what Eddie says. I wouldn't want to lead you astray.

More lightning. More thunder.

'I'll get dressed,' says Eddie.

Cooper is in the kitchen towelling Herman dry.

'Eddie's getting dressed,' I tell him.

Cooper eats a banana and pulls on his jacket and trainers. 'I'm going with you,' he tells Eddie, who appears in the doorway. 'I know the path, but we'll need a torch.'

'This is insane,' says Eddie. 'What was Jack thinking? You gotta look ahead, man. You gotta forward plan.'

This, coming from my brother who, for years, couldn't forward plan clean underwear, but is now, clearly, an organised adult. How things change.

Eddie goes into the workshop and comes out with three flashlights. 'Ellie, stay put,' he commands me. They step into the howling storm and run to Eddie's car. I watch the taillights disappear into the night.

I am left to hold the fort. It will be pitch black on Crangle Pass. Won't that be dangerous? It's strange how any expression of doubt magically multiplies itself. My anxiety levels rocket, and I wonder if I should wake Grandma.

I log onto Eddie's laptop to check the Met Office forecast.

YELLOW WEATHER WARNING
WIND: Strong winds to 60 Kt.
Becoming cyclonic
SEA STATE: Rough
WEATHER: Heavy rain. Thunderstorms
VISIBILITY: Moderate to poor

In other words, not a perfect night for sleeping under the stars. Oh, an email from Dad. That's unexpected.

Dear Ellie,

A few lines to catch up. Mum and I are just about to go to dinner at a hip restaurant on the Lower East Side. We're celebrating great book sales and having a fabulous time. Fin is in the hotel crèche. I would have had more kids if I'd known I could just drop them off at such a marvellous facility!

Hope you're set to have a great weekend and that the weather is sun, sun, sun. Wear a hat and sunblock. Eat fruit and vegetables. Brush your teeth. Stay safe. Have fun.

A barrel full of hugs and love,

Dad xxx

Hi Dad,

Glad you're having a good time. Give my love to Mum and Fin. Not sunny at the moment. We're in the middle of a thunderstorm.

Love, Ellie x

Why are you up so late? It's 8.30 p.m. here, so it's 1.30 in the morning there - way past your bedtime. What's going on?

Nothing. Eddie's gone out to rescue Jack from Crangle Pass, that's all.

What? Why is Jack on Crangle Pass at 1.30 in the morning in a **THUNDERSTORM?** Does Eddie even know where Crangle Pass is? Where's Grandma?

Don't worry. Cooper's with Eddie. Grandma's asleep.

Oh, dear God. Cooper's on this escapade too? Go and wake Grandma, for crying out loud. I need to know what's happening. **NOW!**

~~You're overreacting.~~ OK Dad. Will do.

Thunder. Lightning. Thunder. Lightning.
Cooper has left his smartphone on the kitchen table. It's locked and I don't know the password. I dash off an email to Jack's smartphone telling him Eddie and Cooper are on their way. A few moments later, Jack responds:
Signal weak. Thanx. J
I'm on my way to wake Grandma, but Herman's dancing by the door again. I unlock it and let him out, but he doesn't need to pee. Storms don't bother him – he's just being nosy. He trots to the gate, hoping to catch the scent of Eddie and Cooper on the wind.

'Herman!' I call, crossly. Herman trots back sheepishly. He's just at the door when Tilly appears, quivering at my feet. She bolts. In an instant her little body disappears over the garden gate.

No! No! No!

And that's how it happened. That's how I ran into the night.

When something changes everything

Tilly is running for her life. Down the hill. Along the promenade. Under the cornfield fence. No lamp posts here. It's dark, dark, dark.

'Tilly?' *OH NO.* **'Tilly? Where are you?'** *OH NO.* **'Tilly?'**

Mustn't sound angry. Mustn't sound desperate. Dogs hate that – it drives them away.

'Tilly? Good girl!'

A fork of lightning. ***There she is!*** Wind. Rain. Thunder.
Thunder.
THUNDER.

Scramble over the fence. Nearly tripped. ***Run. Run fast.***
Fast. FASTER!

My legs ache. I can't keep up. I'm running out of oxygen. Breathe. Breathe! *What should I do? Turn around? Go back? Which way? That way? Or that way?*

I'll run as far as Portis Crag.

'TILLY? TILLY?'

I make it to the other side of the cornfield and find the gap in the hedge. Over the stile. It's wet and slippery. I fall – of course I do. Awkward landing. *That hurt!*

'TILLY! GOOD GIRL!' **Bad dog.** ***BAD DOG!***

I can't see her. She's gone. The rocks on Portis Crag are slick. Another fall.

At what point in a crisis do you give up? At what point

do you start to cry? Alone – abandoned - in the dark – in a storm – soaking wet – bloodied.

'TILLY? PLEASE... WHERE ARE YOU?'

Lightning. A small bundle. Cowering. Soaked. Lost. She runs blindly. I sprint and launch. Rough landing, but I've got her. Grab the scruff of her neck. We roll. Drag her against my chest, tuck my knees. Enfold her. She's rigid with fear. Not a bad dog. Not bad. Frightened. Terrified. Poor thing.

'It's OK. It's OK.'

I anchor Tilly against me. Her heart drums against mine. For a few minutes, I am so relieved. The rain isn't cold. It's lovely – like taking a warm shower. We can't stay here though.

I struggle to my feet. I don't have a lead and I can't carry her all the way home. Eddie's car should be near. He will have parked on the Coast Road near the path ascending to Crangle Pass. I'll find the car and wait. Tilly struggles to be free and I wrestle to keep control. *I should have known she would be terrified of storms. I was the one who opened the door. This is my fault.* **MY FAULT!** *She did the only thing that felt right to her. She ran for her life.*

Eddie's car is parked where I thought it would be. *Good!* I wonder how long it will be before I see their flashlights coming down the pass. They're probably still on their climb up.

I lean against the car. Ten minutes later it occurs to me to try the doors. Eddie always locks his car – but not tonight. Relief! I tumble in. A car is like Faraday's cage.*

We'll be safe in here, even if we're struck by lightning. There's a fleece on the back seat and I dry my face and towel Tilly dry. Now, all I have to worry about is Eddie, Cooper and Jack getting off Crangle Pass. I settle down to wait...

The storm howls on. Not far away, Grandma is sleeping. Juna is sleeping. The guests at the Little Egret Hotel will be tucked between Egyptian cotton sheets, just like its website promises. Only Cooper's mum will be awake, cleaning a deserted office somewhere, oblivious that her son is battling the storm on Crangle Pass. My parents will be dining in some restaurant on Lower East Side, wherever that is, grumbling about their troublesome offspring who always manage to ruin a good time. Here I am, their daughter, a girl with a terrified dog, sorry to make mistakes and flout the rules, but so glad that I have this life to live and the will to survive it. *I promise, I promise, I will read the Rule Book when we all get home safely. I will take the rules to heart.*

Come on, Eddie. Where are you?

Eddie was my age when I was born. He thought I would be gross but found his baby sister was the opposite of gross. Thank you for being out there with Cooper and Jack tonight. Thank you for parking your car here and forgetting to lock it. *Thank you for being my brother.* Thanks, Eddie.

I sense movement behind the car. I'm fixated on Crangle Pass so I stare into the darkness imagining ghosts. Forks of lightning strobe Portis Crag. Everything looks organic and threatening.

I'M STARTING TO PANIC.

That won't help. Deep breaths. Stay calm. Soothe Tilly. What does Cooper say? *Always hope for the best outcome.* That helps. Thanks Cooper.

Rain lashes the windscreen, distorting everything I see. After an age, pin pricks of light appear bobbing down the pass. Progress is painfully slow. One beam disappears – they all do – and there's nothing but black, empty space.

I CAN'T BREATHE.

Blackness.

A light bobs and sweeps erratically. Two. Three lights.

Intake of breath. I watch them descend.

Eddie, Cooper and Jack, bent against the driving rain, trudge to the car. I get out and call them.

'Ellie! Are you all right?' calls Eddie, shocked.

'I'm fine.' *Everything's fine. They're safe.*

Eddie demands to know my story. I tell him how I ran after Tilly. He tells me I shouldn't have let Tilly escape – *that's obvious, but hindsight is 20/20* – and I shouldn't have run after her – *it was a judgement call and it paid off.* Then Cooper tells me he thought Eddie had fallen off the cliff when he slipped on the descent. His voice shakes a little. They found him in a ditch, guided by his colourful language.

'I'll have a bruise on my backside the size of Argentina,' says Eddie.

'Sorry,' says Jack, sounding unusually young. 'This is all my fault.'

'It's all right, mate. What else would we be doing on a Saturday night?' says Eddie, laughing.

161

We're in a good mood. Why shouldn't we be? Everyone's safe.

We head to Jack's laugh-a-lot Auntie Maggie's house. She's standing in the porch in wellies, a kagoule over her billowing nightie. She hurries to the car.

'Oh Jesus, Mary and Joseph,' she laughs, poking her head through the front window. 'Thank the good Lord you're all right. Ellie, what are you doing with these crazy boys? Oh, my goodness, I've been worried out of my mind. You, boy,' she says to Jack, 'will explain yourself, but not until morning. I need to face this over caffeine and a couple of pop tarts, or else a slug of Jim Beam, though if take a hit tonight, I'll never get up for the Farmer's Market and I've got my heart set on a bunch of Gladys Pincher's artichokes. Right, you all get off to bed with you. Make sure you towel your hair dry before you turn in or you'll catch a cold. Thanks, Eddie. Oh, is that Cooper? I hope you've not been leading my nephew astray. Probably the other way around! He looks like a cherub, I know, but he can be a right little devil. Anyway, thanks a bunch. That's terrif.'

Laughing, she drags Jack out of the car and marches him into the house. He doesn't seem quite so grown-up now.

'Grief. Auntie on speed,' says Eddie.

'Eddie texted her on our way up,' says Cooper. 'She's had plenty of time to get herself worked up.'

'Good job Dad doesn't know what's going on,' says Eddie to me.

'Yeah,' I say, quietly. Except, Dad does know and, no

doubt, there will be consequences. That flattens my mood a bit.

Eddie says he will drop us off at home and then double back to check the boat.

'We'll go with you,' says Cooper. 'Is that OK, Ellie?'

'Sure,' I say. We'll soon be home and dry and then I can put things straight with Dad.

Eddie turns the car around and heads back. He pulls up on the grass. 'Won't take the car down there in this weather. I'll walk. You sit tight.'

We watch him stride over Portis Crag, join the track and turn down the harbour road.

Tilly whimpers.

'What a night!' says Cooper, exhaling slowly.

The storm rages on. My eyes are trained on the spot where Eddie disappeared. We don't speak. After a few minutes, I sense Cooper's anxiety. He clears his throat.

'I'll go and check he's OK,' he says.

I look at him. He's worried.

'We'll go together,' I say. I hug Tilly. 'I won't be long. Be brave.'

We get out of the car and face the storm. The rain hurts my face. I grab Cooper's hand and, with the help of a flashlight, we pick our way across Portis Crag. There's no point in talking – the howling wind pummels our ears. Instinctively, I know that if the boat needs securing, Eddie can't do it alone. A dim security light illuminates surf crashing over the harbour wall into the car park. We step onto the jetty just as Eddie runs towards us, drenched by a rogue wave.

163

'It's no use,' he shouts. 'It's too dangerous.'

'Will she survive?' asks Cooper, peering down the jetty to where Susie Q heaves and rolls in the swell.

'I don't know. It's not worth the risk,' yells Eddie against the wind. *'Get back! Get back!'*

And that's when I see *something* that changes *everything*. A dim light goes on in the cabin. There's movement inside.

'SOMEBODY'S ON THE BOAT! IT'S EDEN! EDEN'S ON THE BOAT!'

Eddie drags me behind the harbour wall.

'Stay here, Ellie! Don't follow me,' he shouts in my face. 'You too, Cooper. Look after Ellie. Call the coastguard.'

Eddie jams his smartphone into Cooper's hands. He turns and runs down the jetty. A cresting wave swallows him. Moments later he reappears, staggering towards Susie Q.

I break free and race after him.

'EDDIE! YOU CAN'T DO THIS! WAIT FOR THE COASTGUARD!'

My voice doesn't carry. Eddie makes a leap onto the bow of the boat which tips violently with the swell. He slams onto the deck and hangs on. The wind whips around us and I'm lost in the spray. Susie Q shudders and groans against her moorings. Waves crash, tearing her free, her fenders grinding against the boat beside her. She lurches to port side and, for an instant, I see the terrified face of the stowaway. It's not Eden. It's Gilby.

Another wave smashes me, dragging me across the jetty, just as Cooper grabs me, taking me down like an anchor. My face hits the deck. I taste blood.

'There's no signal,' he yells, panicked. We stagger to our feet, running to safety behind the harbour wall. *We've got to get help.*

'Little Egret,' I yell. 'Closest.'

Cooper sets off, running. I follow. *If Cooper fails, I must succeed.*

WE RUN. WE RUN. WE RUN. AWAY FROM THE SEA. AWAY FROM EDDIE. AIR RIPS MY LUNGS.

For everything bad I have ever done, I am truly sorry. For every mistake I have made, I will make good. Let my brother be safe. The sea cannot swallow him.

Cooper gets there first. He hammers his fists against the door. He kicks at it.

'EMERGENCY! HELP! HELP! EMERGENCY!' he screams in blind terror.

Vittori opens the door. Cooper shoves past him and races to the reception phone. 999.

'Coastguard!' he gasps, the words trembling as he spits them out: short sentences, clear directions, concise information.

'Yes,' he says. 'Yes... Yes... Yes...'

Cooper confirms everything they need to know.

He looks at me. 'They've been scrambled,' he says, his voice breaking. 'They're on their way.'

Vittori stands, fists clenched, his whole being saturated with anger.

'How *dare* you!' he snarls, blocking our exit. 'How *dare* you kick the door?'

He heard Cooper pleading for help, and *this* is his

response?

'How *dare* you cause a disturbance? Is that *blood* on the floor? You have no respect, no–'

'Call Liam Flynn. Now! Tell him what's happening,' yells Cooper.

He grabs my hand. We push past him. Vittori is nothing to us. He is useless.

It's easier running downhill. I can almost fly.

WE RUN. WE RUN. WE RUN.

The taillights of an ambulance bump down the harbour road. I am relieved and horrified. Another fall. It's an injury, but there's no pain.

We tumble into the car park, breathless. A woman standing by the ambulance looks at me.

'Is Eddie safe?' I gasp. 'Have you rescued my brother?'

Cooper holds me up. 'Her brother's on the boat. Eddie Booton. And a boy – Gilby Flynn.'

I look down the jetty. The sea heaves. Eddie's boat – it's gone.

'Where is he? Where's Eddie?' I plead.

The woman hauls me into the ambulance. I have no strength to resist. It's bright inside. So is the blood. Bright red.

Cooper's so pale I can almost see through him. I know what he's thinking.

'This is my fault,' I tell him. 'Not yours.'

Blood drips off my chin and there's a gash spouting warm blood from my leg.

'What's your name?'

'Menella Edith Booton.'

'Menella?'

'Ellie.'

'The lifeboat crew are on their way, Ellie,' she says calmly. 'They'll sort it out.'

I believe her. I do. Hope for the best outcome.

She seems busy. 'Hold this, Ellie.'

She presses a wad of gauze to my chin. I hold it in place. Then there's pressure on my leg.

I close my eyes...

Hope for the best outcome.

Hope is the key to survival.

Hope...

I'm floating in the sea with Eddie...

I am...

That's all that matters...

I won't drag this out. We all survived. Eddie has the most commented on injury: a gigantic bruise on his bottom that must be visible from the International Space Station. He also dislocated his shoulder, but people aren't really interested in that. He fought to protect Gilby. We still don't know why Gilby was on the boat.

At the point when Eddie was almost beaten, the RNLI* turned out for us: Dave, Sean, Charlotte, Mike and Sandy. I absolutely adore and love them all. They hauled Gilby and Eddie off poor, stricken Suzie Q, landing Eddie like a big fish. It was brutal. No wonder he's vegan. Eddie's jeans got snaffled somehow, and the RNLI's on-board camera recorded his bare bottom in gruesome detail which some mischievous pixie pixelated and uploaded to YouTube a few hours later. Gilby Flynn didn't have a scratch on him.

Cooper is OK. He was shaky later, and I hugged him – carefully – because my chin is glued together and there are absorbable sutures in my mouth. I've got twelve stitches in my leg. A stitch for every year of my life.

We watch TV. Dad is on an American chat show where topics are treated as a bit of a lark.

'Fancy,' says Grandma. 'My son on the telly.'

'So, Walter, you're an English writer and you're here to promote your books – and that's going well, so I've heard.'

'Yes. Incredibly well,' says Dad, chuffed.

'Meanwhile, back in England, things have gone a bit pear shaped, as you Brits would say.'

'You could say that,' says Dad.

'Your son's just had a near-death experience,' says the host gleefully. 'Tell us the story.'

'Oh my,' says Grandma who's still not over the shock.

'Well, it sort of evolved. I got an email from my daughter, Ellie, telling me my son was rescuing one of their friends–'

'You told *Dad?*' splutters Eddie.

'–who was stuck on the edge of dangerous cliffs in a violent thunderstorm in the middle of the night.'

'It was a casual mention, that's all,' I say.

'Are your children prone to emergencies, Walter? Is this a British thing?'

'Not exactly,' says Dad, carefully. 'My kids have, um, generous hearts. They tend to go the extra mile and sometimes – well, it doesn't quite work out.'

'Is that a compliment?' I ask Eddie, doubtfully.

'I can't tell.'

'I was getting a bit fraught because Ellie wasn't answering the phone, and my mother must sleep like a log.' Grandma tuts. 'So, I called the emergency services and asked them to intervene, and the operator thought I was pulling a stunt – with me calling from New York about a *possible* emergency happening in England – but then *another* call came in and they cross-referenced it.'

'Another call?'

'From a hotel near my home in the UK—'

'That's the call you made,' I say to Cooper.

'—which has a fantastic view of the coastline, and a boy called Eden—'

'Eden?' we chorus.

'—the owner's son, just happened to be looking out of the window and saw some sort of struggle in the harbour where my son's boat is moored – and this young boy had the good sense to call for help.'

'And this struggle involved your son?'

'That's right. His boat had broken free from its moorings and was dangerously close to being smashed up on the rocks with a stowaway on board – a local lad, apparently.'

'A stowaway? This is like a movie! And this happened *after* he'd rescued somebody else from a mountain – all on the same night?'

'Not a mountain, more of a big hill, but, yes, that's right. My son, Eddie, the Action Man. I have three kids. They're always up to something. I call them my Three Bootoneers.'

'They sound like cute kids,' says the host, probably not realising that Eddie is twenty-four.

'Oh man!' says Eddie, clutching a cushion.

'Anyway, the emergency operator put two and two together, alerted the coastguard, and the RNLI – a fantastic organisation of brave volunteers – thank God for every one of them – was scrambled to haul Eddie and the lad to safety.'

'We have a clip of the rescue. It's dramatic, but just a warning to people of a sensitive disposition. Eddie bares more than his soul!'

'Kill me!' winces Eddie.

Eddie's bruised backside, even pixelated, will haunt him forever. He may need therapy. Not to mention that I'll have to face kids at school who love to make bottom jokes.

'He'll need to sit down on a cushion for a while,' laughs the host.

'Poor Eddie, always the butt of jokes,' chuckles Dad.

'Seriously. *Kill me now,*' says Eddie, beside himself.

'And how is he now? Has he recovered?'

'Oh, he's fine. He's been in worse scrapes than that,' says Dad proudly.

He looks a bit overwhelmed. It must be the glitz of being on TV and finding himself a best-selling author, not to mention being the father of a Bootoneer who defied death. He fails to mention Eddie's most serious injury – a dislocated shoulder, now strapped up.

'And what about the boy rescued from the mountain?'

'Big hill. Jack. He's fine.'

'And the stowaway on the ship?'

'Small boat. That's a lad called Gilby. He's fine too, though I'm not quite sure how Gilby fits into this picture,' says Dad.

'Let's give a shout-out to the young hero who made the call to the RNLI. What's his name again?'

'Eden.'

'There you go, folks. Well done, Eden. And the hotel?'

'The Little Egret.'

'Let's make it famous. The Little Egret – a hotel in England overlooking the sea. Is it a nice hotel?'

'Oh yes,' says Dad. 'It's a beautiful hotel with a very rich history. And thank you RNLI. Thanks for fishing my lad out of the ocean. Good job!' Dad gives the RNLI a huge cheesy grin and the thumbs up.

More banter. Then the next interviewee is cued up to make light of life and injured limb. Such is the nature of television.

'Not sure Dad's quite got a handle on what happened,' I say. No wonder Mum gets a bit frustrated with him sometimes. 'You didn't get a mention,' I say to Cooper, apologetically.

'Eddie took the heat for all of us. Anyway, I didn't do anything,' says Cooper, typically low-key. 'It was a good outcome. That's all that matters.'

The rest is up to me

Eddie wasn't swallowed by the sea. We are all safe. I promised to make good my mistakes and abide by the rules. I open my desk drawer and carefully take out the envelope.

F.A.O. Ellie Booton

This is your "All Alone and Abandoned" Rule Book.

Yes, we are leaving you but, no, we're not abandoning you, and you won't be all alone. The title is ironic. However, these rules MUST BE FOLLOWED and STRICTLY ADHERED TO, BY PARENTAL ORDER.

Compiled by Walter Booton, devoted dad to three offspring, otherwise known as the Three Bootoneers.

- and Flora Booton, mother of darling aforesaid children.

Also known as Mum xoxox

Oh, my goodness. All this time I have avoided opening

173

this dreaded envelope and inside there's just a wad of blank paper. It isn't a rule book – there's another envelope and inside, a letter, neatly written in Dad's handwriting, and signed by Dad and Mum.

Dear Ellie,

We're leaving you for six whole weeks. It's a long time and we'll miss you, but we know you will cope. Of course we're NOT leaving you with a list of tedious rules to follow – sorry for the tease.

The truth is, unless rules are mathematical or scientific - like $2 + 2 = 4$, or Pythagoras' theorem, or Newton's law of universal gravitation - rules tend to be made up by people to influence or control behaviour. They're not necessarily the same in each country, or even the same in each family.

Here's a good tip: prioritize the rules which protect health and safety. Red, stop! Green, go! Drive on the left (UK). Drive on the right (USA) (Necessary to avoid crashes!) Look both ways before crossing a road and never run with scissors – they're too pointy. Don't dive in the shallow end,

(I did once and nearly knocked myself out) and <u>do</u> brush your teeth - because bad teeth are a health hazard and, oh, so unattractive. You know all of this, anyway.

We know you sometimes feel a bit overwhelmed with rules because you want to do your best and you don't like failing. We all learn rules as we go along and, frankly, they're never ending. Wait till you're doing a Tax Return. Oh, the fun you'll have!

In the meantime, RELAX! You're a good kid. A bit anti-authority - a bit stroppy sometimes - but that's OK. You're spirited. You like to make your own decisions and we support that.

I know we (well, me mostly) tend to over-react. Sorry about that. What we want to tell you is this: WE TRUST YOU TO MAKE GOOD CHOICES.

We trust you because you have values we respect. Values are not like rules. They are not imposed on us. We choose them for ourselves, and these are the values we see in you.

Kindness

Loyalty

Thoughtfulness

Forgiveness

Courage

Compassion

Resilience

Tenacity

We also believe you are humble, so don't let this list go to your head! You're insightful too, so when you get things wrong, you've got the ability to put things right.

For the next few weeks, you'll be on a journey without us, and we know you'll be fine. You have Grandma and Eddie to support you. You've also got wonderful friends. Believe it or not, Eddie will be your best friend and your joint values will see you through. If there are tricky moments, and there always will be, you'll just need to do what feels right. Eddie's instincts have always been good and so are yours.

So, we'll see you in six weeks. Here are two rules

we insist you follow:

1. Do have fun.

2. Do stay safe.

The rest is up to you.

Your loving Dad xxx

And Mum
I suggested a lot of the wording of this letter.
Love you, sweetie
Have a great summer xoxox

True. Your mum has always been the inspiration behind everything I write. She is an amazing woman.

Lost and found

It's a lovely, peaceful evening – the calm after the storm, and we're eating in the garden. I'm chewing very carefully. My jaw is bruised and stiff, and my gums are sore where they've been stitched. I have a wobbly tooth which will need to be fixed somehow.

'You shouldn't have run after Tilly,' says Grandma, looking at me with such love and concern it makes my heart ache. 'You should have come straight to me. We would have worked it out together.'

'I'm sorry, Grandma. I didn't think Tilly would run so far.'

I abandoned the rules I would normally follow. I made mistakes. I don't know if I deserve the trust my parents have in me – but this is what I did, and this is what happened:

Tilly
was terrified
of the storm and did
what felt right to her – she
ran. I ran after Tilly, which
was dangerous and foolish, I know,
but somehow it put me in the right place
at the right time to see a light go on inside a
boat called Susie Q, which was there because my
brother wanted to surprise a girl called Susannah.
I only saw the light because there was a storm, Jack
made a mistake, got stuck on Crangle Pass and texted
Cooper, whose Mum got an unexpected night shift,
which put Cooper in the right place at the right
time to tell me, so that I could tell Eddie,
who would go out into the night, and
be in the right place at the right
time to risk his life to save
a boy called
Gilby.

Without this chain reaction, Gilby might be gone.
Gilby, the boy who caused us so much pain,
is alive because Jack made a mistake,
a dog ran off,
and I have a selfless, courageous brother.

There was a storm.
I ran into the night
and I'm glad.

I walk along the beach with Juna and Cooper. We're quiet and tired. Adventures are exhausting actually. The adrenaline and the worry – it chews you up and spits you out. I'll opt for a quiet life from now on. I'll follow the rules, live my life, stay out of trouble. That's the plan, anyway, but life often gets in the way of a good plan. Elsie's home tomorrow. Her course has finished – it didn't take up the whole summer after all, so we'll meet up and carry on as normal.

Tilly may be going home soon. Mrs Williams has had trial days at home which she's struggled with, apparently. Growing old is always better than dying young, but it's pants sometimes, says Grandma.

We get to the end of the cove. The tide is coming in. Tilly seems preoccupied, but Herman runs into the surf. We climb over the rocks and pull ourselves onto the grassy bank in front of the lighthouse where the summer began. It seems like a year ago.

'Want to sit here?' asks Juna.

'Let's go to see Susie Q and hang for a while,' says Cooper.

I don't want to. I don't say it out loud but, surely, Cooper of all people can read my thoughts. Hands in pockets, he ignores me and strolls on ahead.

Is this what it means to be down? When breathing feels like work? Tilly is determined to follow Cooper. She looks at me beseechingly and pulls on her lead. On Portis Crag we stand at the top of the harbour road looking down at the jetty. Susie Q, a little battered and bruised, is securely tied up. The incoming tide rocks her gently, as if to sleep.

'Can we stay here?' I ask. 'Don't quite fancy going down there.'

'Sure Ellie,' says Juna, like the sensitive soul she is.

We pick our way across Portis Crag and sit down on a slab of rock. Cargo boats dip over the horizon and, closer, a fishing boat chugs its way out to sea. It's peaceful enough. I take deep breaths.

'Don't be afraid,' says Cooper quietly, his little finger touching mine.

'I won't be,' I say. *I'll feel better soon, I'm sure I will.*

The light dims. The wind is picking up and a sea fret begins to roll in.

'We better get home,' I say. 'It's gloomy.'

The dogs stand, ready to move. Herman's kind eyes search mine. He's getting old. He won't live forever, I know, but how can my life be the same without him?

When it's my time to go, you'll have the best memories of me, Ellie, he tells me. *Eddie's safe. We didn't lose Eddie, and as long as I live, I'm here for you.*

My throat is tight and peppery. Tears spill down my face. This is awful. *Awful.*

'Oh, Ellie,' says Juna sympathetically.

Flashback. Wind, tearing and ripping. Heaving sea. Rain, slashing relentlessly, making me feel there's no escape from water.

We lean in together. I'm lost between them and cling, not sure the earth is solid enough to stand on. For a moment, fear screams through me. **LIFE!** There are no guarantees. *Deep breaths.* The warmth of Cooper's shoulder – the pressure of Juna's hand – seeps into my bones. We are together and holding on.

I open my eyes. The windows of the Little Egret hotel wink as lights go on inside. And then I see something magical. Perched on top of the weathervane, in a swirl of mist, an actual little egret is poised to take flight.

'Look!'

It launches itself and we watch as it wings its way along the cliff edge and melts into the stormy sky.

'That's symbolic,' says Cooper. 'Little egrets are always a good sign.'

The dogs are restless. Tilly strains against her lead and barks. Below our gaze, by the edge of the cliff, something moves.

'What's that?'

'I don't know.'

Something shapeless and flowing seems to hover in the mist. Herman's hackles rise and Tilly is focussed.

'That looks... ghostly,' says Juna.

'It's *not* a ghost,' insists Cooper.

We pick our way across Portis Crag. Herman stops to sniff the salty air, searching for clues, but Tilly is desperate. I think of Eddie looking at his watch, getting anxious, wondering where I am. Sure enough, Cooper gets a text.

Are Ellie and Juna with you?

Yes. We're on Portis Crag near the harbour road.

Stay there. I'll come down with Grandma and pick you up.

We strain our eyes. The billowing shape has disappeared. Gone. The gloom has swallowed it.

Cooper phones Eddie.

'We need a flashlight.'

'Are you in trouble?'

'I don't know. We saw something.'

'We're coming.'

And then we hear a cry. How do you describe a sound like that?

'Hello?' I shout.

'Hello?' we shout together.

The dogs pull us forward. It's hard to resist moving towards such a lonely plea for help.

Tilly is desperate to cover ground. She drags us to the place she needs to be. There, crumpled on the ground, is an old lady.

Juna gasps. 'Mrs Williams, are you all right?'

Car lights appear on the Coast Road and swerve onto the grass. Eddie and Grandma emerge in the distance carrying flashlights and Cooper runs over to direct them. In moments, Grandma takes off her jacket and gives it to Cooper who retraces his steps with Eddie.

Juna and I help Mrs Williams to sit up. Carefully, we get her to her feet, a delicate process, complicated by Tilly's manic joy. Cooper wraps the jacket around her frail body. She leans on him for support.

'Amazing grace,' she says. 'I was lost, but now I'm found.'*

Mrs Williams is tucked up in bed in the spare room with Tilly fast asleep beside her. One of her daughters is driving from Exeter to look after her for a while. Grandma is talking to the doctor, and I've managed to earwig their conversation about what happens when old folk are dehydrated: they get confused and may do inappropriate things like wandering about in their nighties, spooking the local community. Grandma drinks plenty, though I've not seen Nanna and Gramps lately. Gramps drinks tea from a big tin mug the size of a swimming pool but Nanna may exist on sour milk from a saucer like Grumpy Cat. I'll call in and see them tomorrow to make sure they're all right.

I earwig again. 'It's amazing Jenny Williams didn't end up at the bottom of the cliff. Your granddaughter and her friends probably saved her life,' says the doctor in a hushed tone.

I open the bedroom door. Mrs Williams is soundly asleep in bed. She looks happy. Tilly raises her head.

'Clever girl, Tilly,' I whisper. 'I know the truth. You rescued all of us.'

Tilly wags her tail. She knew all along her human was out there.

Who did what, when?

We're going to the Little Egret to thank Eden for calling the emergency services. Eddie telephoned Mr Vittori and had a clinically polite conversation with him to arrange it. Cooper and I look at one another. We know what happened at the hotel that night and we've reduced it to one bare fact: there was no mobile signal, so we ran to the Little Egret to call the coastguard. That's it. The confrontation, the blood splats on the floor (my blood, I guess) have been neatly edited out. It's too awful to think about right now.

We pile into Grandma's car: Juna, Cooper and me on the backseat, Eddie, with his right arm strapped up, in the front with Grandma. I'll be so glad to thank Eden, but oh boy, I don't ever want to deal with his dad again.

Alfred is drinking morning coffee on the terrace. He looks startled to see us, and I am reminded that my face is swollen and bruised, and Eddie looks rougher than usual.

'I know, I know. We don't always look this good,' I say, making light of it.

'My dear girl, you are a trooper,' says Alfred. 'And Cooper – what a fearless, loyal friend you are to this family.' Alfred takes Eddie's free hand and shakes it. 'Well done, Eddie. Heroic.'

Don't think you have to make a speech to help someone

feel better. Not many words are needed, just a few of the right ones. Cooper *is* fearless and loyal. Eddie *is* a hero. That's the truth.

'Thanks Alfred,' we say. For an old bloke, he'll be a decent boyfriend for Grandma.

We sit down quietly. The woman from reception delivers Eden like an Amazon package: she has no idea what it is and she doesn't care – she just wants to drop it off.

Eddie stands up and puts out his free hand which confuses Eden, but eventually they settle on an awkward left-handed shake.

'Thanks Eden. You did good,' says Eddie warmly. 'I was like a pair of old jeans on a spin cycle. A few more rotations and I'd have been hung out to dry. You got help there in the nick of time.'

I'm thinking of hugging Eden – then he sniggers and says to Eddie, 'I saw your bum on YouTube,' and the moment passes.

'Of course you did,' says Eddie with dignity. 'It was my unintended gift to the world.'

'Why was Gilby on your boat?' asks Eden.

That's awkward. We don't know. I pull a face and it hurts, but it's enough to distract Eden who wants to see the stitches in my gums. He gives me a five-star rating for grossness. I'm quite pleased. It's the most stars I'll ever get from him.

We sit in the sun and order drinks. There's only so much mileage in a story of life versus death on a dark and stormy night, so the conversation moves on. Eden wants to talk about his latest Nintendo game.

'Oh, I forgot to tell you. I saw your stupid *ghost,*' he says. 'You were in the car with that nutty little dog, and it hobbled behind you. Woo woo! Looked like a mad old lady, if you ask me. *Sooo* scary.'

'Many a true word spoken in jest,' says Grandma.

Poor Mrs Williams. Old, alone and confused – wandering around at night looking for something or someone she couldn't quite find or remember.

No one is young forever. Children grow up. Young people mature with a bit of luck. We aim to survive and grow old, and most of us do. In the end, any one of us could be Mrs Williams: old, ill and vulnerable. I tell Eden all about her.

'Is she the Bitter Regret vandal?' asks Eden, seriously.

'No, Eden,' I say. 'That remains a mystery.'

Afternoon. Elsie's home! Juna and I hurry down the hill to the Box Brownie Café. Elsie rushes out to meet us and we're reunited in a jumble of hugs, jumps and laughter. Maybe now, our carefree summer can begin?

Cooper and Jack stroll up the promenade.

'Elsie's back!' I announce, happily.

'And, let's see – you're *disappointed?*' says Jack.

'No!' I laugh.

Jack gives Elsie a hug. 'Don't believe her, Elsie. She's had heaps of fun without you.'

'It looks like it,' says Elsie, examining my face. I show her the stitches in my leg. She is suitably impressed.

There's a lot to catch up on. We settle ourselves under a

parasol and Cadence brings us a tray of iced drinks. Today is the day we return the keys to the Little Egret hotel. It will be a relief to let this episode go.

'Here's mine,' says Elsie, putting her key on the table.

Cooper sniffs it.

'Yours is brass too,' he says. 'Only the one Eddie found is gold.'

'A golden key,' says Elsie. 'That's *mad.*'

We, the Little Egret Friendship Society, settle down to chat. Jack and Juna lean in together, looking at photos on Jack's phone.

'That's Alex,' I hear Jack say.

'Who's Alex?' asks Cooper.

'My cousin.'

'Let's see.'

We crowd around Jack as he flips through photos. It's funny that I'm more interested in Alex now I know she's his *cousin.*

'She's decent looking. What happened to you, Jack?' jokes Cooper.

There are selfies of me and Jack pulling faces. I can see the contrast between Alex and, well – me – Ellie Booton with the efficient ears.

Then there is the sneaky photo of the second Bitter Regret attack, taken early one morning when Jack was out to capture photos of the sunrise.

'Yikes,' says Elsie. 'That's awful. Who would do such a thing?'

Which brings us to earth with a jolt. We have to make a move. This may be our *last* visit to the Little Egret hotel.

Jack has inside knowledge that the Little Egret letters will be removed today, making way for the new (and boring) Sea View sign.

We walk slowly. It's a perfect day. Gulls bob on the sea like the boats in the harbour. It's hard to imagine that a storm nearly destroyed Susie Q and put us in harm's way. When we reach the hotel, Grandma's car is in the car park. She and Eddie are already here, thank goodness. We find them on the terrace with Alfred, drinking soy lattes. Eddie may well have another vegan convert.

'This is Alfred, Grandma's boyfriend,' I say, introducing him to Elsie.

Grandma looks gobsmacked but Alfred says, 'Thank you for the title of *boyfriend*, Ellie. I am deeply flattered.'

'Well,' I say, a bit flustered, 'You're a bit too old to be a boyfriend, but Grandma's no spring chicken either and, so long as you make her happy, it's all right with me.'

'Thank you. That means a lot,' says Alfred graciously.

Grandma is crimson. I never knew she could turn that colour.

Eddie looks at his watch. 'Right,' he says, 'Let's get this over with.'

Jack's already given his key to Liam Flynn, so he opts to stay behind – the rest of us follow Eddie into Reception. The receptionist phones Mr Vittori to let him know we're here. We sit down and wait. It's quiet – oppressive – like being in a dentist's waiting room. If Mr Vittori accuses Cooper of stealing the keys, I know exactly what I'm going to say, and it won't be pretty.

Cooper is subdued. Juna and I look at one another nervously. On the coffee table is the copy of the Peregrine Post with the story of the Bitter Regret attacks. I turn to page four to read the rest of the article.

Said Mr. Vittori, 'We will not be intimidated. This unpleasant experience has prompted me and my partners to commence a program of refurbishment...'

Blah, blah...

The Little Egret Hotel was built in 1790 for Stephen and Catherine Luxton. Its location, on the hill above the local beauty spot known as Portis Crag, gives sweeping views of the coastline, which worked to the advantage of smugglers. Luxton turned a blind eye, even storing the smugglers' contraband, and duly profited from their spoils. Catherine, renowned for her flowing white dresses, her free spirit and love of nature, created an observation room where she would watch wildlife, particularly birds, and at night, the excitement of the smugglers' activities, often warning them if danger was near.

During the 1800s, little egrets were hunted mercilessly for their beautiful neck plumes which were smuggled into Europe and were more valuable than gold.

Wow! Little Egret plumes were more valuable than gold?

These birds were rare visitors to these shores, occasionally landing on the roof of Luxton Hall, to Catherine's delight. Folklore has it that locals killed the little egrets and traded their plumes. Catherine was heartbroken and refused to allow the smugglers to reclaim their contraband, hidden away in Luxton

Hall's vast cellars. She commissioned a little egret weathervane which was installed on the roof to remind locals of their dastardly deed, and to signal to all birds, they would have her protection. The grand house became known as Little Egret Hall, but sadly, in Catherine's lifetime, little egrets were never seen again. It is said that Catherine's ghost still roams the cliff tops, in a bid to protect her beloved little egrets, which are now regular visitors to this part of the English coastline.

Over the years, the building exchanged hands many times. In 1950, it underwent extensive renovation in keeping with its original Georgian style, and became a luxurious hotel, officially named, Little Egret. The owner was thought to have some dubious foreign ties and, locally, was suspected of criminal activity. He died, taking whatever secrets he had to the grave.

With such colourful history blurred with folklore, it is understandable there have long been rumours of hidden treasure. At one point, it was suspected that the weathervane held the secret, but after examination, it was found to be crafted from burnished copper...

I study the Bitter Regret photo on the front page. Something about it doesn't feel right.

Liam Flynn walks into reception. He looks around – sees me – dismisses me – pulls a big fake smile and heads towards Eddie with his hand out.

Eddie's right arm is strapped up, so Liam Flynn's handshake doesn't happen. He's slightly thrown.

'Hi Eddie,' he says, all pally. 'What are you doing here?'

'Waiting for Mr Vittori,' says Eddie.

'Is this about the keys?'

'That's right.'

'I'll take them.'

'Our arrangement is with Mr Vittori, so we'll wait,' says Eddie politely.

'Why wait? It's a lovely day. Get outside. I can give them to him.'

'That's kind, but we don't mind waiting.'

It's not the answer Liam Flynn wants to hear and he's not happy. Eddie winks at me in a way that tells me not to worry – Liam Flynn will not intimidate us.

Not long ago, Eddie was broken. He listened to songs with doomy lyrics like *Paint It Black*. Now he's in charge and confident. I look at the photo again. I think I know what's wrong.

'I won't be a minute,' I say. Discreetly, I pick up the Peregrine Post and head out of reception to find Jack. He's by the swimming pool with Bella.

'Jack,' I call. 'Can I talk to you?'

He strolls over, reluctantly. Bella, of course, dazzles, but I'm not interested in her. I ask to see the sunrise photo he took with his smartphone of the second Bitter Regret attack.

Thought process:

* Jack's photo of the second attack was taken very early, just after sunrise, probably not long after the hotel was attacked. The shadows are long, and Bella's curtains are drawn.

* The Peregrine Post photo is similar: long shadows, drawn curtains – but the lettering and the paint

splashes are **slightly different**. This photo shows
the **first** attack.
* When the Little Egret was attacked the first time,
Jack was already there when the rest of us arrived.
Bella half opened her bedroom curtains, saw the
graffiti and yelled for her dad, who bounded onto
the scene, saw the damage and was visibly shocked.
* Then Liam Flynn turned up, took control and
started taking photos.
* So, who took the early morning photo but didn't
bother to inform Mr Vittori of the damage? Was it
the attacker?

I hold up the newspaper and point to the front-page photo. I hate to ask Jack this question, but I must.

'Did you give this photo to the Peregrine Post?'

Jack shakes his head and shrugs.

*Why did this story even get printed? Mr Vittori
wanted to keep the attacks hush-hush. So did Liam
Flynn for that matter.

Bella walks over to us.

'Hi Bella.'

'Hello Big Ears,' she says. 'Where's Noddy?'

'Noddy?'

'Yeah. Your dumb friend, Cooper. Funny that you answer to Big Ears, though. I guess it's because you've got ... really big ears.' She sniggers.

Misappropriation of proper nouns. Big deal. Big Ears is an improvement on Smelly Ellie, but Cooper isn't dumb.

Bella: Italian for beautiful. She is, but like the saying goes: *beauty is only skin deep*. I won't spend another second worrying about my ears. What a waste of time that would be.

'Bella, do you know who took this photo?' I ask doubtfully, showing her the Peregrine Post.

She's already bored, but she answers me.

'Are you sure?' I ask, shocked.

'Of course I'm sure.' she snaps.

Jack looks puzzled. He hasn't worked it out yet.

'Thanks, Bella,' I call over my shoulder, running away. *Shame on you for calling Cooper dumb. Shame that your father is a liar!*

Spanner-man is back. He's taking equipment out of his van so that he can remove the Little Egret letters, one by one.

Mr Vittori drives into the car park, springs out of his car and barks orders at Spanner-man: 'Take great care. No damage! I want every nut and bolt. This is my property, do you understand?'

Despite all of the recent positive publicity from Eddie's rescue, Vittori is determined to strip the hotel of its name and identity. The Little Egret must die. He's determined to kill it. It doesn't make sense unless... he has something to gain.

I skirt past Mr Vittori. Portia, the black cat, crosses my path.

'Hey, you!' he calls – but I'm not stopping.

The Little Egret weathervane glints as it shifts in the breeze – but *all that glisters is not gold*. It's a golden decoy, made from burnished copper.

I dip into Reception. Cooper realises something's wrong, but there's no time to explain. I ask them to follow me. Liam Flynn has left the building, but Vittori is closing in. We're out of sight and heading to the terrace before he can notice us.

'What's going on?' asks Eddie.

'I think a crime is being committed,' I say.

Alfred sits on the terrace with Grandma. They are holding hands.

'Alfred,' I say. 'You must listen!'

I've said this before and it's TRUE: adults who listen to children are worth their weight in gold. When I've said my bit, Alfred and Eddie go to speak to Spanner-man, who nods vigorously, tightens the belt around his enormous middle, then packs up his gear and drives off. For now, at least, the Little Egret will live to see another day.

Alfred sits in his car and phones someone he worked with at the tax office, and then he makes another call – to the police. By the time Mr Vittori comes out of the hotel – searching for us – we're heading down the drive; me, Elsie and Juna in Grandma's car, Eddie and Cooper in Alfred's. We pass Jack, sat on the side of the swimming pool with Bella. He doesn't notice us.

Hidden in plain sight and why Dad is not a dentist

The first time I laid eyes on the Little Egret hotel, red paint dripped down the wall like blood. The sign was vandalised – it screamed, ***BITTER REGRET*** – a sinister warning to all who passed over its threshold – a red flag if ever there was one.

After the second attack, and even with all the secrecy, the story appeared in the Peregrine Post. *'I have no idea why anyone would do this,'* complained Mr Vittori. Poor man! The hotel had been targeted. People were jealous of his success. It was *so* unfair. Some people accepted Mr Vittori's assessment that, yes, maybe, it was time for the hotel to be given a new identity. Not me. It didn't feel right.

When Bella told me it was her dad who took the sunrise photograph appearing in the Peregrine Post, I knew he was manipulating us. It didn't fit the timeline. Hours after he'd taken that photo, he pretended he was seeing the attack for the *first* time. I almost felt sorry for him. Then I lost sympathy because he was so obnoxious – shouting at us, accusing us of vandalism. What a horrible man! Cooper and I stood up to him and I'm glad we did – because his shock wasn't real. He was faking it! He underestimated us – children – who see things, think things – have opinions and make decisions. His mistake was to share *that* photo with the Peregrine Post. It was clumsy. A mistake. Or maybe he thought he was too clever to be caught. *He* attacked the Little Egret. *Twice.*

There is an investigation and Mr Vittori and Liam Flynn have been asked all sorts of awkward questions. Alfred says they both seem to have had criminal intent, though not necessarily working together. Liam Flynn was doing his own thing. When Gilby was questioned, he admitted his dad had ordered him to befriend Bella, so that Gilby could snoop around the hotel and steal anything valuable that would fit in his pockets. Trouble is, Gilby liked Bella and seems to have had an attack of conscience. Oh, the irony. Gilby told the police he stole the key (and other items) but didn't know it was gold until his dad got excited about it – then he tried to return it to Bella by dropping it on the beach. He was going to pretend to find it and give it back – but then a huge, *savage* dog *(Herman? pur-lease!)* bounded over and covered the key in sand.

Liam Flynn was livid that Gilby had *'lost'* the key. They rowed about it – and Liam threw his son out of his car. Award him *Dad of the Year!* It's actually a very sad story. I never thought I'd say this – but we all feel sorry for Gilby. His life, from the outside at least, is a gilded cage.

Alfred sits with us in the evening sun eating spaghetti. He's a very tidy eater. I'm not. Eating is still tricky and sauce drips down my chin onto my T-shirt. Normally, I

197

would be mortified, but Alfred seems like family now. Cooper – well, Cooper's part of our family too. And Juna. And Elsie.

'Vittori heard the hotel had some hidden gold. He has partners, all dodgy types, who helped him buy it so they could take the hotel apart, piece by piece. He's actually not that well off. He really is a puffed-up peacock with a few loose bum feathers.'

'Alfred!' says Grandma.

'Sorry Ruby. That's unfair on the peacock, I know,' says Alfred, apologetically.

He's loving these titbits of gossip his ex-colleagues feed him. We're sworn to secrecy, of course, and I know it's safe in my journal.

'He planned to remove and inspect *all* the fixtures and fittings – the door handles, the light fittings, the *hotel sign*–'

'*Especially* the hotel sign,' I say.

I'd better explain.

Question:

How do you hide gold in plain sight?

Answer:

Like the song says, you **paint it black**.

'Yes,' says Alfred. 'That bit of insight was *amazing*, Ellie. Homing in on the bloody sign. Well done!'

Grandma tuts. Alfred's not used to moderating his language around kids. It's quite entertaining.

'Sorry, Ruby,' says Alfred. 'My bad.'

'Actually, Grandma, Alfred's right. The sign did look

bloody after it had been attacked,' I say.

'Well, you've got to give Vittori credit for the *Bitter Regret* graffiti,' says Grandma. 'What a sly, cryptic way to start a dialogue with the locals about killing the Little Egret hotel.'

'Don't praise him, Grandma, *pur-lease.*' I say. 'Mr Vittori is a complete and utter twonk.'

Grandma arches one eyebrow. I know that look. So does Alfred.

'Sorry Grandma. My bad,' I say, nudging Alfred, who chuckles.

Catherine Luxton was full of bitter regret when the little egrets were killed. It's a heart breaking story and it gave Vittori the dastardly idea to attack his own hotel so that he could kill it off and plunder it. *Shame on him!*

Would you be interested to know that all the letters of the Little Egret sign have now been removed by the police? Except for the G and the R, they were all cast in gold and they're worth a **FORTUNE!**

Gold, hidden in plain sight, probably stolen long ago and definitely **NOT** declared to the tax man. Who would have thought it?

It's 9.00 p.m., or 4 o'clock in the afternoon in New York, USA. Eddie and I are waiting for Mum and Dad to Skype us. I've changed my T-shirt and brushed my hair. Their call comes through and I answer it.

My parents squeeze into the screen. Dad's arm is around Mum.

'Hello Bootoneers,' says Dad, cheerfully. 'Have you

managed to secure your underpants, son, so the world can settle back on its axis?'

'Walter!' says Mum frowning. 'It wasn't funny at the time. We were beside ourselves with worry—'

'But in hindsight,' Dad chuckles, 'it cracked us up.'

'Will you ever let me forget this?' asks Eddie.

'Sure son. As soon as you start paying rent.'

'For goodness sake, Walter,' says Mum. 'He's been paying rent for years.'

'Has he?' asks Dad, genuinely surprised.

'Cash in hand to Mum,' whispers Eddie to me.

'Never mind,' says Mum. 'How are you, darling girl?'

'I'm fine,' I say. I tilt my chin, so she gets the full effect of my injury. 'Do you want to see my gums?' I pull down my lower lip and lean towards the camera.

'Oh my,' says Mum, grimacing. 'You took a tumble, that's for sure.'

'And *that's* why I'm not a dentist,' shudders Dad, backing away.

Eddie and I chat to our parents. Their trip has been a success and now, they just want to come home. They're missing us, apparently. It has *nothing* to do with wanting to supervise us – nothing at all.

'I read the Rule Book,' I say, finally. 'Thank you for your letter.'

'What letter?' asks Eddie. '*I* didn't get a letter.'

'Mum and Dad said they trusted me and that you would be my best friend. Oh, and that your instincts have always been good –'

'Really? They said that?'

'–and that if there were tricky moments, we should just do what felt right.'

Validation. There are moments in life when you need to hug. We've been through a lot together, Eddie and me. I wrap my arms around Eddie's neck and bury my face in his tangled hair. Eddie holds me tight. When I look back at the screen, Mum is dabbing her eyes. Dad gives her a squeeze.

'Can't wait to get home,' says Dad, sounding a bit choked.

Fin pops up, as sticky as ever.

'Oh God. Don't dribble on the keyboard,' says Dad, smooshing Fin's face with a wipe.

'Hi Fin,' we call to him.

'Who's that?' Mum asks Fin.

'Eddie and Mellie,' says Fin. 'That's my *bwufa* and *sista*.'

The simple rules of friends and biscuits

The sea is calm, the forecast is good. Jack walks as far as Portis Crag with us. He's on his way to the Little Egret to see Bella and Eden. Their life has been knocked sideways with police swarming around the hotel, asking their dad questions he doesn't want to answer.

'Tough. Actions have consequences,' says Jack, a little harshly.

'But it's not their fault,' I say, defending Bella and Eden.

'It's not yours, either,' says Jack.

I swallow. I feel guilty. Unravelling a mystery is one thing – affecting people's lives is another.

'Vittori's been shady for a long time,' says Jack. 'He was always gonna get caught. He's not a good guy.'

We study one another. Jack clears his throat.

'I made a prat out of myself,' he says. 'That Crangle Pass thing – it was insane.'

'To put it bluntly but accurately,' says Cooper, without malice.

'I'm sorry.'

Jack hugs me and I'm grateful. I don't like the tension there sometimes is between us.

'You're imperfect – like the rest of us,' I tell him.

And that's the best way to be. Honestly, it is. Imperfection saved Gilby's life.

'You may be right,' says Jack.

I watch Jack walk away. It doesn't hurt me. I'm glad we're friends.

'I hope Bella's OK. Say hello to Eden for me,' I call after him. I don't know if Bella and I will ever be friends, but life can sometimes surprise you.

We pick our way across Portis Crag. Gilby sits on the wall in the same spot where Abigail sat the day she kicked Herman. I'm surprised to see him – we all are – and it's obvious he's uncomfortable seeing us. *Bullies, please note – it's not worth it – the tables always turn. Gilby is on his own – looking lost – and we're the ones with friends.*

'Hi,' I say.

'Hi,' says Gilby. He doesn't look up. He jumps off the wall and starts to walk away. I glance at the others. Elsie is pale. She was the one who suffered the most at Gilby's hands. Juna was pushed around by him too.

Herman sniffs the air and wags his tail. He doesn't understand people who don't automatically love him. What is *wrong* with this human? He's a Labrador after all. He's *Labradorable!* He trots past Gilby and turns to confront him – tongue out, tail wagging, with a look of such honesty and trust, I could cry.

Gilby is frozen.

'You're not good at reading body language, are you?' I say, going to Herman and clipping on his lead. 'He just wants to be friends, that's all.'

'Wouldn't know much about that,' says Gilby.

He's not the same boy. He's flattened.

'I'll be with you in a mo,' I call to Cooper, who signals to

Elsie and Juna to walk on. I still don't know why Gilby was on the boat that night, but it might have something to do with the relationship he has with his father.

'Are you all right, Gilby?' I ask. It's sad to see someone's life in such darkness.

'Sure,' he says bitterly.

No eye contact. There is so much wrong to put right, I don't know what to say. Silence. It's awkward, but sometimes it serves a purpose. My thoughts are there, just out of reach. Why are some things so hard to understand – even harder to explain?

'We all need to say sorry sometimes,' I say out loud, thinking of my parents who have struggled to be happy together – of Eddie and Susannah – of Elsie and me. I smooth the gravel with my foot.

'Does it work?' he asks. He's weary.

'Saying sorry? Sometimes. If you mean it.'

Herman looks up at me. He was a puppy when I was born, and he is my oldest friend. Herman has never done anything wrong, but he's always ready to say sorry. Herman loves me completely, will never hurt me and will leave a hole in my heart when he leaves me. I drop a kiss on his head. He's thrilled – but why doesn't Gilby love him too? Herman nudges Gilby's hand.

'He thinks in terms of friends and biscuits. If you haven't got a biscuit, you'll have to be his friend.'

'I don't think so.'

He turns away.

'It's a rule.'

'Don't be stupid.'

'The *biscuit or friend* rule. Haven't you heard of it?'

Herman wags his tail hopefully.

'You can join us if you want,' I say, though I know it's too soon.

'No thanks.'

I turn to go. 'Oh,' I say, remembering Bella getting in my face. 'What did you tell Bella about me?'

I wait, but Gilby is good at withholding information. I give up and start to walk away.

'I told her you were... OK.'

Are you kidding me? Bella wanted to slap me for being OK?

Gilby clears his throat. 'You stand up for your friends. You're a decent person. So is your brother.'

That's more than I expected. I turn to face him.

'Eddie's great,' I say and mean it. 'I aspire to being adequate.'

Gilby manages a small smile.

'Maybe another time, Ellie,' he says, using my name for the first time.

'Sure,' I say, not feeling sure. I can be hopeful though. I can hope for the best outcome for all of us.

Gilby strolls away, head down, hands in pockets. An aimless, lonely day is not a good day. Like Grandma's book on loneliness says: have a plan, socialise and have at least one trusted person in your life. So far, my day is textbook perfect.

I catch up with the others.

'Is he all right?' asks Cooper.

'He looks awful,' says Elsie, concerned.

'I believe, one day, Gilby will apologise.'

Elsie and Juna link arms. 'Well, if he ever does, it will be a start,' says Elsie.

A fresh start. People need that sometimes.

We make our way along the jetty and climb aboard Susie Q. We've brought food – of course we have. We pack it away in the galley, replacing the biscuits. I don't think Eden ate them. I think it was Gilby, hiding away from the misery of his life.

Cooper and I climb back on the deck. Susie Q, securely moored, rocks gently against the tide. Eddie's shoulder will take weeks to heal, so for now, sailing's out of the question. On the hill, the Little Egret weathervane glints golden in the sun.

'Are *you* all right?' asks Cooper, picking up a mop to clean the deck. He always contributes – always helps.

'I'm decent,' I say. 'Gilby said so.'

'Everything about you is decent,' says Cooper.

He wasn't injured that night, but stuff got into his head. He hates that Eddie and I got hurt, I know he does.

'Cooper...' *How do you thank someone who helped you stay alive?* 'I would have been washed off the jetty if you hadn't pushed me down.'

Cooper leans on the mop. I understand his body language – I've seen it in Eddie.

'I'm sorry,' he says. He squeezes his eyes shut. He shouldn't regret what he did. It was instinctive. It was necessary. It was so brave.

I reach up and put my hands on his shoulders. He knows what I'm thinking – he always does. *We survived.*

It was the best outcome – and that's everything we could have hoped for. I'm not afraid of Susie Q, or the sea. Thank you, Cooper. Thank you. Thank you.

'I like my scar. It stops people from focussing on my ears.'

'Your *decent* ears,' says Cooper.

A true friend is worth their weight in gold. No. They're priceless. They're loyal, kind, and brave when they need to be brave. A true friend will save you.

Two little egrets skim our heads as they busily flap their way along the coast.

I call to Elsie and Juna. 'Come and see this!'

This is our life. We're here to see little egrets find the light and fly free. It's a good day.

Signing off – a little bit older and wise enough, thanks to Cooper, to hope for the best outcome. Love and thanks to all my friends.

Thank you, Elsie, for putting hurt behind you and for sharing secrets only true friends can share.* Thanks, Cadence, for being Elsie's mum.

Thank you, Juna, for loving animals as much as you love your friends. I know how pure that is.

Thanks, Jack, for being both sensible and foolish. That makes me feel better about myself.

Thanks Mum and Dad for trying to work things out. Thanks for understanding how rules make me feel trapped sometimes. I need to make my own decisions, but I *will* go to school, do my homework, brush my teeth (of course I will – who wants rotten teeth?) and wait until

I'm seventeen to learn to drive. (It's different in other countries – which goes to show that rules aren't universal.) Thanks, Mum, for letting me know I am your *darling girl*. I will help you want to wear orange every day. Thanks, Dad for telling me that all stories must have truth. I have taken that to heart.

Thanks, Fin, for being cute and sticky - which doesn't limit your potential, believe me. You are the opposite of gross. (That's a compliment.)

Thanks, Grandma, for being brave enough to start dating. I love that your old age has young bits in it, because I need you so much. Good luck, Alfred. (Heads-up – cool it with the opera - Grandma prefers jazz.)

Thanks, Liam Flynn, for showing me how much I prefer Grandma's biscuit tin on wheels to your flash BMW, any day of the week – and, Dad, I appreciate you all the more because you're nothing like Liam Flynn.

Thanks, Mr Vittori, for setting examples I will always remember and never follow. Thanks, Bella, for encouraging me to feel comfortable in my own skin. You probably didn't mean to, but you helped me.

Thanks, Abigail, for showing me that effort doesn't always produce results, but that's OK. I tried, and I haven't given up yet.

Thanks, Gilby, for helping me reassess what an enemy is. I understand you a bit more. I want you to be happy. Truly, I do.

Thanks, Tilly, for running away. You are a fey, brave and loyal dog. Thanks Mrs Williams for loving Tilly so much she found you.

Thanks Susannah, for being honest with me in the end.* Enjoy your travels and then come home and tell me all about them. *Please.*

Thanks, Eden, for calling the emergency services. Thank you. *Thank you.* I don't care that you give me two stars for my looks – thank you for making that call. You did a great thing.

Thank you RNLI for every moment of your service. You are **trustworthy, courageous, selfless and dependable.**

Eddie, you thought I might need you and I did. Thank you for being brave enough to jump and strong enough to hang on. Thank you for being there. So glad you're my brother.

Cooper... You seem to learn things the hard way, so I don't have to. You're not the boy I first thought you were. Never judge a book by its cover – good saying – because you amaze me, and, because of you, I'm alive to be amazed. Thank you, Cooper. Thanks.

And thank you Herman - the most imperfectly sound of all sentient creatures in my life - for your lifetime of friendship and love, your ability to live in the moment, to never hold a grudge, to laugh when you're running through the surf, and to find joy in a biscuit. You teach me something new every day and I love you.

Ellie x

Extra Jots

The full Peregrine Post report
MYSTERIOUS ATTACKS ON LOCAL HOTEL

Reporter: Olive Stephens

During the night, the Little Egret Hotel was targeted by an act of vandalism. The hotel sign was defaced with red paint and altered to read, *Bitter Regret.* This is the second such attack in one week. Co-owner, Vincent Vittori commented, "I have no idea why anyone would do this. We are the proud new owners of this hotel and I know there is certainly no reason, now, nor in the past, for patrons to ever regret, much less bitterly regret, their stay here. The standard of our accommodation and service is second to none and as far as we are concerned, it is business as usual." [*Continued on page 4*]

[*Continued*] PR Consultant, Liam Flynn, a local man advising the hotel's owners, has recommended upgrades to the hotel's security, including the installation of closed-circuit television, which is currently being undertaken. Said Mr. Flynn, "It is unfortunate that CCTV was not operational at the time of the attacks. My client is badly shaken, and we feel these wanton acts of vandalism may have been motivated by jealousy, as the Little Egret has an enviable reputation along this coastline."

Said Mr. Vittori, "We will not be intimidated. This unpleasant experience has prompted me and my partners to commence a program of refurbishment. We envision a streamlined, updated and even more luxurious feel to the hotel, whilst still making the most of its beautiful Georgian features."

The Little Egret Hotel was built in 1790 for Stephen and Catherine Luxton, and was originally known as Luxton Hall. Its location, on the hill above the local beauty spot known as Portis Crag, gives sweeping views of the coastline, which worked to the advantage of smugglers. Luxton turned a blind eye, even storing the smugglers' contraband, and duly profited from their spoils. Catherine, renowned for her flowing white dresses, her free spirit and love of nature, created an observation room where she would watch wildlife, particularly birds, and at night, the excitement of the smugglers' activities, often warning them if danger was near.

During the 1800s, little egrets were hunted mercilessly for their beautiful neck plumes which were smuggled into Europe and were more valuable than gold. These birds were rare visitors to these shores, occasionally landing on the roof of Luxton Hall, to Catherine's delight. Folklore has it that locals killed the little egrets and traded their plumes. Catherine was heartbroken and refused to allow the smugglers to reclaim their contraband, hidden away in Luxton Hall's cellars. She commissioned a little egret weathervane which was installed on the roof to remind locals of their dastardly deed, and to signal to all birds, they would have her protection. The grand house became known as Little Egret Hall, but sadly, in Catherine's lifetime, little egrets were never seen there again. It is said that, in heavy sea frets, Catherine's ghost still roams the cliff tops, in a bid to protect her beloved little egrets, which are now regular visitors to this part of the English coastline.

Over the years, the building exchanged hands many times. In 1950, it underwent extensive renovation in keeping with its

211

original Georgian style, and became a luxurious hotel, officially named, Little Egret. The owner was thought to have some dubious foreign ties and, locally, was suspected of criminal activity. He died, taking whatever secrets he had to the grave.

With such colourful history blurred with folklore, it is understandable there have long been rumours of hidden treasure. At one point, it was suspected that the weathervane held the secret, but after examination, it was found to be crafted from burnished copper.

It may come as a shock to local people that there are plans to change the hotel's name to symbolise a fresh start. Said Mr. Vittori, "Due to this unwelcome and negative publicity, we feel it is necessary to change the hotel's name which will involve, unfortunately, removing the sign on the front of the building and the little egret weathervane. Locals and patrons need not worry. The Little Egret's demise means the birth of something even better."

* Susannah

I'd love to tell you that Susannah and Eddie are back together. That hasn't happened. Susannah finds it hard to trust – and I don't blame her. She's been let down by her family, which makes her doubt people. When Eddie chose not to travel with her, she thought it was because he didn't really love her. He had his reasons to stay, and I'm glad he did. Susannah only realised Susie Q was a boat – not a girl he'd fallen madly in love with – when she saw Eddie's bare backside on YouTube. Ironic really, as Eddie bought the boat as a surprise for her, thinking he and Susannah would sail into the sunset together. She's teaching yoga in Cyprus now. Sometimes she emails me and when she does, Eddie tells me to give her his love. We carry on with our lives, enjoying the good bits, helping each other through the iffy bits, and hoping that everything will work out just fine for everybody.

* Paint It Black and Susie Q

Paint It Black is a song written in 1966 by Mick Jagger and Keith Richards, members of an ancient group called The Rolling Stones. Believe it or not, Grandma's a fan and introduced Eddie to this music when he was about five. I like the song, *Susie Q*, which is happier, and was covered by the Rolling Stones. It was written by Delmar Allen Hawkins (known as Dale Hawkins) and Robert Chaisson and was first recorded in 1957. Other people are also credited as co-writers.

* Don't tell me Grandma is about to go AWOL* as well?

In case you didn't know, AWOL is an acronym for *absent without leave*. It's a military phrase for someone who legs it without permission, intending to come back when they can be bothered. All right, I know. Grandma does not need my permission to do anything. I'm over that demanding phase of my life. I think.

* Loneliness

I never really understood that Grandma might be lonely until I came across her book: *Alone But Not Lonely: 100 Rules for Solo Living.* You can be lonely in a crowd, if you're missing someone or something you feel you need in your life. Did you know that elderly people who feel lonely are nearly twice as likely to die prematurely than those who do not feel lonely? Loneliness hurts people and it can affect anyone at any age. That's why friends are so important. Good friends – people you can trust and have fun with. Mum was lonely, even though she's married to Dad. Dad was lonely – because they'd stopped being best friends who had fun together. They're working on that and I think America has been good for them. I am hopeful. So are they.

* Elsie Mabel Berry-Brown
Elsie did explain Berry-Brown to me and also told me about her dad. It was in confidence, so unless Elsie tells you, you won't hear anything from me. That's what friends are for. We are the jugs that thoughts, secrets, fears, wishes, hopes and dreams are poured into by the people who trust us most. I have jug ears, apparently, which makes me an ideal confidante.

* Abigail
Abigail, whose dad just so happens to be a policeman who has strict rules on what kids should and shouldn't do, got up to no good. That story is told in Journal No. 1. She's a hard person to get to know.

* Gilby Flynn
I wrote about Gilby in Journal 1 and 2. It all started off when he called me Smelly Boots and I called him Filby Glynn – a tame response, considering. Bullies find it hard to let go and he was determined to become my arch enemy. If you're sane and sensible, all you want from bullies is their absence from your life. For various reasons, Gilby keeps popping up in mine.

* Eddie's in loco parentis.

Loco parentis, you'll know, is Latin for 'in the place of a parent.' If Eddie becomes an actual parent one day, I will comb his baby's hair. I love Eddie – he's a local hero now – but he's not passing on his hair habits to any niece or nephew of mine.

* PC Jennings once accused Eddie of vandalism, but that's another story.

This story is in Journal 1. I'll give you a hint – it was the middle of the night and Eddie was attacking things with a crowbar.

* 'What's this fascination with you and keys?'

Cooper is thinking of something I did in Journal 2. It was dodgy and he will never let me forget it.

* I'm thinking of the time when I snooped and found the 'I ♡ U' message in the lighthouse.

This happened in Journal 2. I still don't know who that message was for.

* 'All that glisters is not gold.'

You'll know all about Shakespeare, an English playwright, poet and actor, who died over 400 years ago. He wrote 39 plays, including The Merchant of Venice. 'All that glisters is not gold,' is a line from it. Cooper tried to explain the plot to me and I needed to lie down in a darkened room afterwards – it was so gruesome and complicated. Nutty, unfair rules don't make life easy, that's for sure.

* 'He's late,' I say, 'for a very important date.'

Referring, of course, to the White Rabbit in Lewis Carroll's classic story, Alice in Wonderland. Eddie read me this story when I was seven, before he got the hang of deodorant. I loved the story so much, I put up with Eddie's smelliness.

* Faraday's cage
Michael Faraday was an English scientist. In 1836 he realised that his cage distributed electrostatic charges (like lightning) around it, and kept things in the cage (like people) safe from being frazzled. A car behaves like a Faraday cage, thank goodness.

* RNLI
The Royal National Lifeboat Institution was founded in 1824 with the purpose of preventing loss of life at sea, and saving lives at sea. The RNLI provides a 24/7 lifeboat search and rescue service and seasonal lifeguards. Their work is driven by *values* and the volunteers are expected to be **trustworthy, courageous, selfless and dependable.** These are pretty cool values.
The RNLI rely on donations and fundraising to do their work.
Their website is: rnli.org

* 'Nothing is certain in life except death and taxes.'
I googled this. A bloke called Daniel Defoe first wrote about *death and taxes,* but it was Benjamin Franklin, an American jack of all trades, who wrote a letter in 1789 saying, "...in this world nothing can be said to be certain, except death and taxes." What a cheery thought.

Fun fact: Benjamin Franklin invented the lightning rod.

*Amazing grace. I was lost but now I'm found.

Grandma says this is a line from her favourite hymn. It was written by John Newton who died over 200 years ago. He was a British sailor who worked on slave ships but later became an Anglican clergyman, writing poems which became hymns. One of the lines of this hymn is, 'I was blind, but now I see.' Grandma says he finally saw how wrong slavery was. He lived to see the UK's abolition of the African slave trade in 1807, just before he died. Even now, the world is full of modern slaves. We should never accept something so wrong.

* HMRC

If you didn't already know, I'm sorry to tell you that HMRC stands for, Her Majesty's Revenue and Customs, a government department that collects taxes. If you earn enough money, you give some of it to the government and they spend this tax money for you on stuff like roads, schools and healthcare. Alfred's advice on tax is 'suck it up and pay' - whatever that means.

* Jane Austen, Persuasion

My mum loves this book. It's about a woman called Anne who falls in love with Frederick. She's persuaded (or manipulated) to tell him she can't marry him, mainly because he's too poor. He's bitter and she's full of regret. Years later, when he's rich, she bitterly regrets her decision. I'm not a fan of bitter regret. Cooper's right – always hope for the best outcome and try to nudge life in that direction. That's good advice.

*KIMBILIO, the Swahili word for sanctuary

The UK registered charity, Congo Children Trust, runs Kimbilio, a sanctuary for vulnerable children and young adults in Lubumbashi, DR Congo. The children in DR Congo often end up working in slave conditions, on the streets and in mines.

In 2017, Sky News journalist, Alex Crawford, filmed children in DR Congo labouring in cobalt mines. Kimbilio offered a home to two brave boys, Richard and Dorsen, featured in Alex Crawford's film, but thousands of children still need help. If you use goods powered by rechargeable batteries, including smartphones, laptops and electric cars - the cobalt in the batteries may well have been mined by children.

FACT: Children labouring in cobalt mines can work a 12 hour day for as little as 8p. Sometimes they earn nothing – which means they often go hungry. These children work in dangerous, exhausting conditions. Many children have no education.

At Kimbilio, children are nourished and nurtured; they learn practical skills and experience education. It is a place away from the exploitation of the mines and the misery of surviving street life. Kimbilio is a safe place where children are given hope for their future.

Congo Children Trust: congochildrentrust.org

Flinty Maguire

Flinty Maguire lives at the coast in North Yorkshire, England, with her husband and her mum. She has two dogs: a golden Labrador who loves to paddle and eat – well, anything really – and a quirky rescue fluff-ball who, after a traumatic start to life, lives to adore and be adored. There are also rescue hens in the family, and long may they cluck.

After seeing Alex Crawford's heartbreaking film featuring Richard and Dorsen, child cobalt miners in DR Congo, Flinty became a voluntary worker and supporter of the charity, Congo Children Trust, which runs Kimbilio, a sanctuary for vulnerable children. Richard and Dorsen are now supported by Kimbilio and Flinty has had the privilege of chatting to them over the Internet.

Congo Children Trust is building a school. Education gives children choices and hope for the best outcome for their lives. Profit from sales of this book is donated to the Kimbilio school project.

flintymaguire.com